"Luke, are you sure? You know so little about me."

"You can tell me the rest on the way to Athens." He leaned nearer and kissed the pulse in her neck.

Caprice moaned as his lips blazed a trail of aching desire up the column of her throat. "Luke," she whispered with longing in her voice, "I love you so much."

"Are *you* sure?" His voice was velvety as he nuzzled her ear. "I don't want to rush you."

"I know I love you with all my heart. I have no doubts about that."

"Good. Because when we get married, I want it to be forever."

"Forever?" she gasped. How could she keep her background a secret for the rest of her life?

Dear Reader,

If you're looking for an extra-special reading experience—something rich and memorable, something deeply emotional, something totally romantic—your search is over! For in your hands you hold one of Silhouette's extremely **Special Editions**.

Dedicated to the proposition that *not* all romances are created equal, Silhouette **Special Edition** aims to deliver the best and the brightest in women's fiction—six books each month by such stellar authors as Nora Roberts, Lynda Trent, Tracy Sinclair and Ginna Gray, along with some dazzling new writers destined to become tomorrow's romance stars.

Pick and choose among titles if you must—we hope you'll soon equate all Silhouette **Special Editions** with consistently gratifying romance reading.

And don't forget the two Silhouette *Classics* at your bookseller's each month—reissues of the most beloved Silhouette **Special Editions** and Silhouette *Intimate Moments* of yesteryear.

Today's bestsellers, tomorrow's *Classics*—that's Silhouette **Special Edition**. We hope you'll stay with us in the months to come, because month after month, we intend to become more special than ever.

From all the authors and editors of Silhouette **Special Edition**,
Warmest wishes,

Leslie Kazanjian
Senior Editor

LYNDA TRENT
Beguiling Ways

Silhouette Special Edition

Published by Silhouette Books New York

America's Publisher of Contemporary Romance

SILHOUETTE BOOKS
300 East 42nd St., New York, N.Y. 10017

ISBN: 0-373-09457-4

First Silhouette Books printing June 1988

Printed in the U.S.A.

LYNDA TRENT

started writing romances at the insistence of a friend, but it was her husband who provided moral support whenever her resolve flagged. Now husband and wife are both full-time writers of contemporary and historical novels, and despite the ups and downs of this demanding career, they love every—well, *almost* every—minute of it.

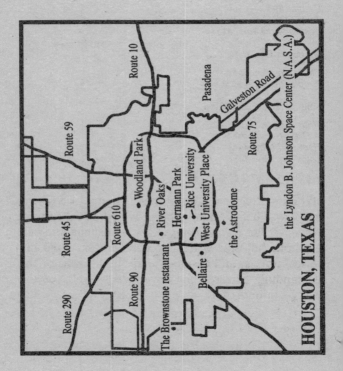

HOUSTON, TEXAS

Route 10

Route 59

Route 45

Route 290

Route 610

Route 90

Woodland Park

River Oaks

Hermann Park

Rice University

West University Place

Bellaire

The Brownstone restaurant

the Astrodome

Pasadena

Galveston Road

Route 75

the Lyndon B. Johnson Space Center (N.A.S.A.)

Chapter One

Caprice Dolan stepped out of the cool movie theater
and breathed in the hot, muggy air of Houston. The
lights of the marquee glistened off her pale, red-gold
hair. Her sister Katie and her seven-year-old niece
Heather followed her out into the night. A few blocks
away Caprice could hear freeway traffic, and on the
far side of the parking lot across the street she could
hear the passing sounds of a teenager's deafening rock
music. The music faded away, and when the traffic
light turned green, the threesome continued toward
Katie's station wagon.

"Can you imagine living like that?" Caprice said.
"All those jewels and furs and that gorgeous house!"

"The wonders of Hollywood," Katie replied. "I
don't think anybody is really that rich."

"Some people are," Caprice insisted. "The Banning family lives right here in Houston. Why, Luke Banning alone is worth millions, and there's no telling how much his sister and parents have."

"But is he happy?" Katie asked sagely.

"Everyone always assumes that the rich and famous can't possibly be as happy as the average person. Hogwash! If I had millions, I could figure out how to be happy."

"What's hogwash, Mom?" Heather spoke up.

"Yeah, 'Mom,' what is it?" Caprice teased.

"Eat your popcorn," Katie told her daughter.

Heather handed her the red-and-white box. "I don't want any more. I'm not feeling good."

Katie touched the girl's forehead and frowned. "You feel pretty warm."

"It's a hot night," Caprice suggested hopefully.

"But we just came out of an air-conditioned theater. Feel her face."

"She does feel a bit feverish."

Caprice exchanged a look with her sister over Heather's blond head. "Maybe it's something she ate."

"I don't feel good," Heather repeated.

"She ran a fever a couple of days last week, too." Katie's voice was tinged with worry. They both knew there wasn't enough money to take Heather to a doctor, but if she was really sick, they would have no choice.

"Let's get her home and put her to bed," Caprice said, stroking the child's silky hair. "I guess we overdid it by coming to the movie. I just thought dollar night was too good to pass up.''

"Coming to the movie didn't make her sick,'' Katie reassured her sister. "She never really got over whatever she had last week.''

They walked toward the old station wagon, both adults more worried than they were admitting. Heather hadn't been well for months.

Behind them, Caprice heard the approaching slap of running shoes on the concrete sidewalk. She moved aside for the jogger to pass, and as he did, he grabbed the strap of her purse and increased his speed to a dead run.

"Hey!'' Caprice shouted, and started to run after him, but her high heels were no match for his rubber soles. "He stole my purse!''

"Oh, no!'' Katie looked around the emptying parking lot. "Do you see a policeman?''

"Never mind, he's gone now. Damn! I really liked that purse.''

"How much money did you have in it? Why aren't you more upset?''

Caprice shrugged philosophically. "He stole a secondhand purse, a tube of lipstick, a comb and thirty-eight cents. I didn't even have my driver's license in there. I just wish I could see his disappointment when he opens it. Now, if it had happened tomorrow after I got my paycheck, I would have chased him down, heels or no heels.''

Katie shook her head. "Still, I think we ought to report it.''

"There isn't much point in it. All I saw was a hand and a jogger in a gray sweat suit. Do you know how many gray sweat suits there are in this town?"

"How many?" Heather asked.

"Too many," Caprice said with a laugh as they reached the car.

Katie unlocked the door, and Caprice wrestled it open, letting Heather slide in first. She was more upset than she let on, but she didn't want her anger to further ruin their night. An evening at the movies, even on dollar night, was a rare treat, and Caprice wanted to salvage the romantic mood. She knew Katie, like most people who had very little, valued her few possessions; the loss of even inconsequential belongings would disturb Katie for weeks.

Katie got in behind the wheel, and on the third try, the engine started. She jiggled the knobs of the air conditioner, but only hot air belched out. "I think it's given up the ghost. Roll down your window."

Caprice could feel the heat from Heather's warm body next to her on the seat, and she knew the girl's fever was rising. "I'll stay up until Heather feels better," she said. "You have a busy day tomorrow."

"So do you."

"No more than usual. Mrs. Walters is coming in for a fitting, but she's easy to deal with. You have that bon voyage party to cater." As the car picked up speed, the warm breeze through the window began ruffling Caprice's hair, so she twisted it and pushed it behind her back to keep it from tangling. Suddenly she leaned forward. "Stop the car, Katie! Stop the car!"

"What!" Katie slammed on the brakes, as she automatically reached over to keep Heather from falling forward.

Caprice jumped out and hurried to the curb. Returning triumphantly, she waved an object over her head. "It's my purse! He must have looked through it, then tossed it aside." She got back into the car and examined her bag in the overhead light. "He kept the thirty-eight cents. Oh, well, I have the purse back." She smiled at her sister and niece. "Maybe this is a sign that our luck is about to change."

"Good. We could use it."

Katie lived in the Heights, an older residential area northwest of downtown Houston between Interstate 10 and the Loop, in one of the houses that no one would bother to renovate. The small frame structure was neither charming nor nostalgic, and it had no interesting possibilities. Thus, the rent was cheap. It sat on a narrow street between other houses of the same type. Each one, including her own, was in need of paint and repair. Several months after Katie's husband, Jed Farnell, had vanished, Caprice had moved in to help make ends meet. For more than a year now, they had managed to keep the house and pay the bills, but there was not enough money for extras—like doctor's visits or medical insurance. Naturally, after Jed's disappearance, the insurance he had had through his employer lapsed. Though the insurance company had offered Katie an opportunity to convert the group medical policy to an individual one, and Caprice encouraged her to get the coverage, Katie turned it down because it was much too expensive. Although she admitted that Heather had not been a healthy child, she argued that her daughter's illnesses had never been serious, and with the money she would save in premiums, she could pay an occasional medical bill. But an increase in rent and unexpected car repair costs had quickly taken their toll on their budget. After Heather's first bout with the mysterious fever, Katie reconsidered the need for insurance, but the premiums for even minimal coverage were astronomically high, and not one policy covered a preexisting condition. Now Heather was sick again, and there was no money to spare.

After Katie had put the girl to bed, Caprice said, "Maybe I could get a second job."

"You work long hours as it is. Even you have to sleep sometime."

"Heather needs to see a doctor."

"I know it!" Katie snapped. "I'm sorry, Caprice. I'm just so worried about her. This isn't the flu or a cold. I think she's sick with something bad. Damn Jed! The bastard! Why did he have to take off like that? I need him!"

"No, you don't. If Jed were here, he would be off drinking with his buddies. He never gave you a dime of his paycheck if he could help it."

Katie sank down onto the worn sofa. "I know. But at least he was *here*. You've never been married, Caprice. You don't know how it is to share a house with a husband, to have a man to talk to and sleep beside. You don't understand what it's like to have a husband one day and him just take off the next. Do you think he'll ever come back?"

"He always has before."

"He's never been gone an entire year though."

Caprice didn't answer. She secretly hoped Jed was gone forever. His drinking and gambling and skirt-chasing had turned her against him years ago, and she was pretty certain Jed could become violent if he were pushed. But all he ever had to do to win Katie over was to give her that boyish grin and promise never to do it again, and Katie was full of forgiveness. Caprice couldn't understand it. True, she had never been in love, but she could see through a man like Jed Farnell. With his handsome looks he was probably some woman's gigolo—it wouldn't be the first time. "Go to bed, Katie. I'm not sleepy yet. I'll watch over Heather and see that her fever goes down before I go to bed."

"I'm not sleepy either."

"Yes, you are. I saw you yawning on the way home. I'll wake you if she gets worse."

With a sigh of tired resignation, Katie got up and stretched. "You talked me into it."

Caprice went into the tiny kitchen and made herself a cup of instant coffee. She could use the time to draw up some ideas she had for evening gowns and casual dresses. Her employer seldom used her sketches, but if she did, Caprice was given a bonus. It was very late by the time Caprice went to bed.

By morning Heather's temperature was back to normal, though she said she wasn't feeling much better. Katie worried about leaving her, but she had no choice. To save on gasoline, Caprice dropped off Heather at the sitter, then took Katie to the Sunny Day Caterers, before driving downtown to Swayse's.

Mrs. Swayse frowned at Caprice when she arrived, glancing pointedly at her watch. "You're late."

"I'm sorry. My car nearly refused to start and the traffic was heavier than usual."

"You've lived in Houston all your life. Surely you're used to traffic by now."

Caprice didn't answer the barb. Her employer was rarely in a good mood, and it was best simply to ignore her. She put away her purse and offered her sketches to the tight-lipped woman. "I drew up some new designs. Are there any here that you'd be interested in?"

Mrs. Swayse took the sketches as if she were doing Caprice a favor and perused them with her sharp, glittering eyes. "I don't see anything spectacular here. These are all rather unimaginative."

"What about this one? Look how I designed this sleeve. That's not bad."

"*Designed* seems rather egotistical for a mere seamstress. At Swayse's we turn out only the best. We aren't interested in 'not bad.'"

With great effort, Caprice bit back her retort. She couldn't afford to anger the woman. There was still a chance she might take one of the ideas and the bonus would pay for Heather's appointment with a doctor. Mrs. Swayse ruffled through the sketches again and shook her head. "Very pedestrian. These are no better than the last ones you gave me. If I were you, I'd stick to putting in hems and leave the designing to those who know how."

The sharp words stung Caprice, and she was glad the woman had turned away to file her sketches in her desk along with the others. She didn't want her employer to know her barbs had hurt her so. The designs were very good, and Caprice knew it. If Mrs. Swayse would give them a chance, she knew they would be popular. When the doorbell announced that a customer had entered, Mrs. Swayse pasted a professional smile on her lined face and quickly stepped out front. Through the doorway, Caprice caught just a glimpse of June Walters's plump figure, which was about as much as she ever saw of any of Swayse's clients. Mrs. Swayse took the alterations down herself, and Caprice and the other seamstress were given the dresses to alter.

Instead of sitting down to work as usual, Caprice went to the desk where Mrs. Swayse had put away her sketches. If her employer wasn't going to use them, there was no reason to leave them sitting in a drawer. Caprice took out the new sketches, but she was surprised to find the old ones were gone. On the bottom of the drawer was a key.

Caprice picked it up and glanced nervously over her shoulder to the door in the back of the workroom that was always kept locked. She had often joked with the other seamstress that this must be where Mrs. Swayse hid the bodies of her former employees. As she thoughtfully fingered the key, the side door opened, and Sara, the other seamstress, came rushing in. Caprice was startled, but relieved that the intruder wasn't Mrs. Swayse.

"I'm late. Is Swayse here?"

"Is she ever! I was late, too, and she's in a particularly bad mood."

"All her moods are bad. What's that?"

"It's a key. I found it under my sketches."

Sara grinned. "I'll bet it opens that door back there. Let's see."

"We can't do that. If she wants that door locked, she's the boss."

Sara peeped into the showroom. "She's busy with Mrs. Walters. Come on." She took the key from Caprice and went to the back door.

"It's probably just a storeroom," Caprice whispered as Sara turned the key. "There's not much else it could be."

Sara opened the door and flipped on the light switch. Inside the small room was a rack of dresses. "It's just more clothes," Sara said in disappointment.

"What did you expect? Seamstresses' bodies?" Caprice glanced at the nearest dress, then caught the door as Sara started to shut it. She pushed that dress aside and looked at the next, then the next. Cold anger started to chill her bones. The dresses were very familiar, and with good reason. They had been made up from the sketches Mrs. Swayse had "rejected."

The color drained from her face, and she shook off Sara's hand when her friend tried to caution her. Every one of the dresses were from Caprice's designs and some were pinned as if Mrs. Swayse was in the process of altering them. Names pinned to the garments told Caprice that many had been sold to prominent women in town.

"What are you doing in there!" a severe voice demanded.

Caprice spun about to see Mrs. Swayse bearing down on her. Sara was trying to appear to be hard at work in the sewing area behind a pile of dresses. "You stole my designs," Caprice accused in a frosty tone.

Mrs. Swayse drew herself up and clamped her thin lips together. Caprice grabbed a dress from the rack and brandished it beneath the woman's prominent nose. "You stole my ideas and sold them as your own!"

"Get out," Mrs. Swayse finally managed to sputter. "Get out! You're fired!"

"Fired! I quit!" Caprice was too furious to realize what she was doing. "You actually stole my designs!"

"Don't you dare accuse me of any such thing! *I* designed these clothes! No one would believe a snippy little seamstress could do this!"

"Sara, you saw my sketches," Caprice said. "Are these my ideas or not?"

Sara looked up, her eyes full of misery. She needed the job too much to be honest. "I'm not sure. No, no, they aren't," she blurted out as she turned red.

Caprice glared at her, then wheeled around to Mrs. Swayse. "They are, and you both know it! I'm calling the police."

"If you can't prove it in court, you had better think twice," Mrs. Swayse said with a nasty smile. "Do you have copies of these sketches you allege I stole? Can you prove you thought them up? I rather doubt it." Moving quickly to her desk, she scribbled out a check and thrust it at Caprice. "Here's your pay for the last two weeks. Now take it and get out."

Caprice grabbed it and stuffed it, along with her new sketches, into her purse. She didn't trust herself to speak, and Sara was studiously avoiding her eyes. Caprice grabbed her purse and flounced out into the side street, taking great pleasure in slamming the door behind her. She was shaking so hard she had trouble getting the key into the lock on her car. When she was seated in the baking interior, two scalding tears coursed down her cheeks. Caprice angrily brushed them away. She hated to cry, and she didn't dare examine the fact she had actually been fired. Without her salary, she and Katie would have a difficult time indeed.

Caprice coaxed the protesting car to life and eased out of the parking space. Tonight she could cry over Mrs. Swayse's duplicity. Right now she had to find a job. She edged into Houston's downtown traffic and began to drive among the towers of steel and glass.

By late afternoon she was hot and so tired she ached all over. Every store she had tried either didn't have an opening for a seamstress or was leery of one with no references. She knew better than to tell them what had happened at Swayse's; no one would be willing to trust their designs to a person who had been fired from her previous job over a dispute about designs.

Caprice picked up Heather, then went to get Katie. She dreaded telling them that she no longer had a salary to help support them.

Katie hurried out to the car and leaned in the window. "I hate to ask you to do this, but could you possibly help out tonight at a wedding reception? Jo Nell called in sick and Mr. Haynes needs someone to work.

You and Jo Nell are about the same size. You could wear her uniform.''

"I don't know, Katie. I've never done any catering before, and Heather..."

"I called Betty Parkinson, and she said she'll watch Heather. This is the Banning wedding and the pay is good.''

Caprice sighed. Under the circumstances, she couldn't afford to turn the job down. "Okay, I'll do it."

"Great! Come inside and get Jo Nell's uniform before Mr. Haynes finds someone else for the job. I'll teach you all you need to know on the way over to the house."

Heather was deposited with Katie's friend while Caprice showered and put on the brown and white uniform. She looked at herself in the mirror and shook her head. Because she was slimmer than Jo Nell, the uniform bunched around her middle and the skirt was an inch too long. Katie had never been a good judge of size, nor was the uniform designed to be flattering. She stepped into Katie's extra pair of sturdy brown shoes and knelt to tie them, ignoring their drab appearance. She wasn't there to make a fashion statement.

Caprice rolled her thick hair into a bun and pinned the ruffled cap over it. She didn't bother to put on makeup; Katie had warned that Mr. Haynes liked his workers to be as inconspicuous as possible.

By the time they reached the River Oaks addition, Katie had taught Caprice enough of the art of serving the wealthy for her to get through the night. As they drove through the gates, Caprice checked her cap to be sure it was straight. The Bannings' house was a huge colonial-style mansion that sat far back from the street. The expansive lawn was an emerald carpet of well-manicured grass. Numerous shrubs including azaleas and camellias had been carefully placed to accent the magnificence of the house. The towering live oaks and magnolias were in perfect proportion to the three-storied home. Caprice, who had never seen such a fine house at such close range, unabashedly stared as Katie drove around to the back and parked the car. Together they passed through a small yard, and entered the home through the servants' entrance.

The rest of the caterers from Sunny Day were already there and the chef was in a frenzy over the temperature of his canapés. Caprice edged around him and followed Katie to the front of the house. Everyone was still at the wedding so the house was relatively quiet. Caprice looked around at the expensive furnishings and exquisite prints and floral arrangements. Overhead hung a huge chandelier that was adorned with hundreds of pieces of sparkling crystal, and the luxurious Aubusson rug beneath her feet cushioned her footsteps. Despite its elegance, however, the house felt unwelcoming. It was more like a color photograph in a magazine than a home.

"I didn't know Luke Banning was going to get married," Caprice whispered to Katie. "Imagine living in a place like this as a bride."

"This isn't his house, it's his parents'," Katie whispered back. "And it's not his wedding, it's his sister's. You know, Christine Banning and Winston

Norwood. I served at one of her engagement parties, remember?"

At their request, the butler unlocked a massive rosewood china cabinet and removed two silver trays before relocking it. Caprice raised her eyebrows as they exchanged a glance. Katie was accustomed to cabinets under lock and key, but this was all new to Caprice.

"Don't they trust their own staff?" she whispered as they carried the trays into the dining room.

"I don't think the Albert Bannings trust anybody. I've been here before, and they keep everything locked up."

Mr. Haynes was busy recounting the bottles of Dom Perignon and barely nodded to his new waitress. Suddenly the sound of automobiles pulling into the driveway could be heard, and in moments a crowd of elegantly attired, laughing wedding guests was streaming in through the front doors. Dispassionately, Mr. Haynes popped the cork on the first bottle of chilled champagne and poured it into crystal stemware, inspecting each glassful as he went. After placing the glasses on the trays, he motioned for Caprice and Katie to begin serving.

Caprice threaded her way into the crowd, never speaking or making eye contact, and being very careful not to spill the champagne. She knew many of the guests from glimpses she'd had of them in Swayse's, though they didn't know her. Everyone was in high spirits, and there were jokes and gossip and flirtations exchanged throughout the room. Caprice found herself listening with interest to who was seeing whom

and which ones were contemplating a trip and to
where. She saw why Katie, who had an avid interest in
gossip, enjoyed her job. No one paid any attention at
all to the women serving the champagne, and Caprice
was beginning to think she really was invisible.

All her life Caprice had had a secret fantasy. As a
child she had pretended she was a foundling princess
being raised incognito and that someday she would
come into her own. When she was a teenager, she had
dreamed of becoming a highly successful designer and
being fabulously rich, or perhaps that she would meet
a prince, who had *not* been raised incognito, who
would sweep her away to a castlelike house. Even as
recently as a month before, she had planned what
would happen if she could just get her designs in front
of the right person. Now she was rubbing elbows with
Houston's crème de la crème and trying not to douse
them with champagne in the process.

When the bride and groom arrived, the toasts began and Caprice had to work even harder to see that
the empty glasses were removed and fresh champagne
was served.

Christine Banning-Norwood was as naturally blond
as the beauty salon could make her, though her tanned
skin hinted at darker hair, and she was as thin as good
health would permit. Her groom looked somewhat
dazed by it all, and seemed content to come and go as
his bride bade him. The Norwoods were almost as
wealthy as the Bannings and this marriage was something of a royal match.

As Caprice was making her way back from the
kitchen with a trayful of champagne, a man who had

just arrived came rushing across the foyer and Caprice had to step back to avoid a collision. As he brushed by her, Caprice's lips parted in awe. For a moment, she was so captivated by his appearance that she forgot why she was there. This was a man to rival the prince of her girlhood dreams. In fact, she had never seen such a handsome man in all her life. His hair was as dark as midnight, and his shoulders were so broad she was sure that his impeccably tailored coat had been custom-made. He was tall, too, and moved with a muscular, pantherlike grace. She wasn't the only one to notice him; his entrance was causing almost as much of a stir as had the bride and groom's. He went to Christine and bent to kiss her cheek before shaking Winston's hand. "Welcome to the family," he said to the groom.

"Luke," Christine said with a note of disapproval and a hint of chastisement. "You promised to be on time for my wedding!"

Caprice edged closer to hear him say, "I'm sorry. We ran into bad weather in the Gulf, and it made us late. *Idlewild* is no match for a tropical storm, it turns out."

"You should know better than to take a yacht out on a stormy day," someone beside him said. "It's dangerous."

Luke Banning shrugged. "I was in Ixtapa and had to get back for the wedding. I decided to chance it. I knew if I didn't show up, Christine would be harder to face than any storm. Where's the champagne? I haven't toasted the happy couple!"

Caprice pushed the tray forward, and as he turned, she got a good look at his eyes for the first time. They were a clear gray and they seemed to see right into her soul. For a moment, she felt as if the two of them were alone in the room. Then he looked away and the spell was broken. Caprice lowered her eyes hastily before he could look back and catch her still staring at him.

"To the bride and groom," he said, lifting his glass and smiling at the new couple. His teeth were startlingly white in his tanned face.

Caprice backed into the anonymity of the crowd. She could feel Mr. Haynes's eyes on her, and she knew she must remain in the background, but at the same time something within her cried out for Luke to see her and somehow recognize her. Of course, that was impossible. He had never seen her before in his life, nor had she seen him. He was Luke Banning and she was nobody at all. For some reason, however, he still seemed to touch some chord deep within her and trigger a memory that had been forgotten before she was born. Caprice melted into the crush of bodies and put the entire room between her and this fascinating man.

Chapter Two

Jobs were scarce in Houston, and the summer heat was enervating. Caprice forced herself along the miles of pavement, leaving résumés at every business that would accept them. None, however, was encouraging about her prospects. By the end of the week she was thoroughly discouraged.

Heather had not improved, so when payday came around, Katie took her to a doctor. After a series of tests, the news wasn't good. "He says it's her liver," Katie told Caprice as she put her purse down on the kitchen table.

Caprice looked up from the bowl of corn bread batter she was mixing. "Her what?"

Katie nudged Heather toward the bedroom. "Go on to bed, honey. I'll look in on you in a minute." The girl nodded languidly and left the room. Katie looked back at Caprice. "It's a disease of the liver. I can't even pronounce it." She showed Caprice a slip of paper on which the doctor had written the name of the disorder—biliary atresia.

After wiping her hands on a kitchen towel, Caprice took the paper and tried to make some sense out of the words. With worry lines creasing her brow, she sank down onto a chair. "Is it serious?"

Tears welled in Katie's eyes, and she looked away as she ran her fingertips over the scarred surface of the table. "Yes, as a matter of fact, it's very serious. She doesn't know. I just couldn't tell her."

"Katie, sit down and tell me exactly what the doctor said."

"He ran all kinds of tests and asked every question you can imagine. He says she was born with the problem, but it's just now becoming obvious." Her voice broke, and she sat down as she squeezed her eyes shut and trembled with the effort not to sob aloud. "I can't even pronounce the name of it, Cappy!"

Caprice covered her sister's hand comfortingly. "Did he give her medicine?"

"Oh, yes! The pharmacy is going to love us."

"How long will it be before she will be well?"

Hot tears seeped from the corners of Katie's eyes, and she shook her head vigorously.

Deep dread knotted Caprice's stomach. "I don't understand."

"He said," Katie explained as she gulped a lungful of air, "that there is no cure."

"What?" Caprice could only whisper the word, and she felt suddenly cold and sick.

"He says the only hope is for Heather to have a liver transplant."

Outside the window Caprice could hear children playing and a lawn mower growling. On the stove a simmering pot of pinto beans was filling the little house with the aroma of supper. These were smells and sounds that she had known all her life, but none of them seemed real. "When?" she asked in a choked voice.

Katie again shook her head. "He couldn't say. The sooner the better, of course, while she's still strong." Her voice cracked, and she drew a tortured breath as she clasped her trembling hands together on the tabletop. "She could possibly go as long as a couple of years without it. He says it varies with each child."

Caprice didn't know what to say. This was so unexpected that she was stunned. "A lot can happen in two years. They might find a cure or . . ."

"He said *maybe* two years. It could be a matter of months. They don't know yet. I have to take her to a specialist in a couple of weeks to see if there's any change."

"We'll get through this," Caprice said. "Together we'll manage to raise the money."

"It's two hundred thousand dollars!" Katie groaned. "Two hundred thousand! Where are we going to get money like that?"

Caprice sat back, her mouth dropping open. "Surely you misunderstood the amount."

"No, I didn't. And do you want to hear the real clincher? We have to have half of it up front, or they won't even consider her for the operation!"

All the color drained from Caprice's face. "Give me the doctor's number. That can't be right."

Katie shoved her a crumpled piece of paper with the doctor's name, address and phone number. She sat miserably at the table while Caprice went to the phone in the other room and had a terse conversation with the doctor. When she came back into the room, Katie glanced up, her eyes red and her face swollen. "There's no mistake, is there?"

Slowly Caprice shook her head. "I can't believe it. He says the hospital board sets the policy. A hundred thousand has to be paid up front. Nobody has that kind of money on hand. He said the balance could be made in payments, if our credit was good."

Bitterly Katie barked out a laugh. "Only the rich have the option of healthy children. When you're poor you have to sit back and watch..." Her voice broke off and tortured sobs rocked her.

Caprice put her arms around Katie and patted her as their mother had done for them when they were children. Anger and determination gradually replaced Caprice's initial shock. Her eyes were painfully dry.

"We aren't going to give up, Katie. Not on this! One way or another, we're going to find the money."

"How can we possibly do that? We can barely make ends meet as it is."

"The March of Dimes or somebody must help out people like us. I'll call everybody in town. Maybe we

could put up our furniture and the car as collateral to
get a loan from a bank.''

"Yeah, for maybe a thousand dollars, if the banker
were blind!''

"Don't give up. We won't quit without even trying.
Miracles still happen.''

"You read too many books. They don't happen to
people like us.'' Katie's voice was dull and bitter. "Not
a half hour's drive from here there are people who
throw away more money than that on frivolous luxu-
ries. Why couldn't we have been born like them? It's
so unfair! That's what gets me. It's all so damned unfair!''

Caprice let Katie vent her frustration while she
racked her brain for a solution. Maybe there was a way
of getting Heather's name on a list for some club to
sponsor her medical treatment. Maybe the specialist
would even waive part of his fee in view of their circumstances. Katie was no good at negotiations so Caprice decided she would accompany them to Heather's
next appointment. She was just as stubbornly proud
as Katie, but Heather's life was at stake. Under these
circumstances Caprice was willing to do anything.

Luke Banning parked his white Maserati in front of
his sister's French provincial mansion and strolled over
the perfectly manicured lawn. At this time of day he
knew she would be out by the pool so there was no
need to go inside. As he had expected, she was
stretched out on a recliner beside the turquoise water.

He dipped his hand in the pool and dribbled cool-
ing droplets onto her thin, brown middle. Christine

shrieked and jumped. "Luke! You scared me half to death!" she complained as she lay back down and wiped the water off her stomach. "Look what you've done. You washed away my tanning cream."

"So much sun isn't good for you," he said as he sat beside her in a lawn chair.

"I'll be the one to worry about that."

She applied a liberal amount of cream to her stomach and again arranged herself on the recliner.

"Where's Winston?"

"He went downtown. A stockholders' meeting or something. Are you staying for dinner?"

"Not tonight. I'm flying to Saint-Tropez for a week or so and my pilot is meeting me at Intercontinental in a couple of hours."

"Are you really going there? You ought to head for the Alps and get out of the heat."

"I can't. This is a business trip. I gather you enjoyed your honeymoon in Zurich?"

"Of course. Winston found a marvelous chalet with a splendid view. We're thinking of buying it and going there every summer." She waved her hand to discourage a small fly. "Goodness knows I'd love to escape this humidity."

"If you dislike heat so much, why do you lie out here?"

"Tanning salons don't tan quite like the sun."

"Then why tan?"

"Don't be ridiculous, Luke. Nobody wants to be pale and look washed out. You've heard what Dee Dee Allen calls it—shop clerk's pallor."

"Dee Dee isn't the kindest of people and if you ask me, her skin looks like leather."

"Nonsense. She's no darker than I am."

Luke tactfully didn't comment. He looked across the pool to where workmen were toiling behind a knee-high hedge. "What are you doing over there?"

Christine opened one eye. "We're putting in a cro-quet lawn."

"I didn't know you played."

"I don't, but Winston has decided to take it up. We stayed a couple of days in Bordeaux because Winston has such an interest in wines and while we were there, he dabbled in the game a bit, and decided he wanted a lawn of his own."

"It looks as if they've staked out an Olympic pool."

"It's no bigger than two tennis courts. You have to sterilize the soil down to about four feet to really get rid of the weeds. Before they fill the hole back in, they'll lay in a drainage system. Naturally the dirt will be mixed with sand to make the soil more porous."

"That should prove interesting. That black gumbo clay they're digging in will sift the sand right out through the cracks in the hot weather."

"Not if the drainage system is laid out on a stone flooring. See? Winston has thought of everything."

"It's a rather expensive toy, but I guess if it makes him happy, he's welcome to it. Personally, I'm going to stick to tennis and racket ball."

"Well, what good is money except to spend?" his sister said offhandedly. "Who are you taking to Saint-Tropez?"

"No one but myself. I told you it's a business trip."

"Really, Luke, you ought to think about settling down."

"Spoken like a happy bride. No, I've tried that and it wasn't for me."

"*Paulette* wasn't for you. Besides, that was two years ago."

"Just the same, she made a lasting impression on me."

"I think she was just after your money. I was glad to get her out of the family," Christine said. "That's what you get for marrying a Dupree. They're so nouveau riche."

"At the time you were all for it," he reminded her. "You seem to have twenty-twenty hindsight."

"At least I don't have to worry about *my* marriage falling apart. I've known Winston all my life. He's perfect for me."

Luke smiled. "I hope you're right. Mother and Dad couldn't stand another divorce."

"They hate scandal—who doesn't? Paulette was very stupid to be so open with her affairs. Why, she practically had them pick her up at the house!"

"An affair is an affair whether it's public or private. If there is one thing I won't stand for, it's lying."

"You always were like that," she mused, "even as a boy. I wonder why. I'll bet my analyst could help you."

"No thanks. I don't want to get over it. If I ever settle down again it will be with someone I can trust."

Christine laughed. "Good luck."

Luke stood up and looked again at the hole being dug beyond the hedge. He shook his head. Winston was full of ostentatious ideas, but this one topped them all. Although Luke had a friendly relationship with his sister and her new husband, he had very little in common with them. "I've got to be going."

"Fly carefully," she said in their usual farewell, "and don't talk to strangers."

"One out of two isn't bad," he responded with a grin. "Tell Winston I said hello."

He left the way he had come. Although Christine and Winston had been married only a short while, they had lived together for nearly a year, and Luke was no stranger to the grounds. A big Doberman, ostensibly purchased as a guard dog, trotted up to him and nuzzled his hand affectionately. Luke paused to stroke the animal's head and patted its muscular rib cage. "Good boy, Newport. You're a real tiger, aren't you?" The dog wagged his short tail and licked Luke's hand.

As Luke got into his car and drove away, he wondered if he would ever remarry. Paulette had hurt him far more than he had ever let on. Luke knew he was too trusting. He always had been. He tended to believe in the people he cared for, even when it was clear to everyone else that he shouldn't.

Someday, he thought with characteristic optimism, he would find someone who was perfect for him, and when he did, it would be forever. He would see to that. In the meantime he was willing to suffer through Christine's well-intentioned matchmaking and his mother's thinly veiled suggestions that it was his responsibility to carry on the Banning name.

* * *

"Jo Nell quit her job," Katie said over the phone. "If you get right down here, Mr. Haynes says you're hired. You can buy Jo Nell's uniforms cheap."

"I'm on my way!" A few weeks earlier Caprice would have turned down a job with her sister's employer, but now she was more than happy to wear the drab Sunny Day uniform.

That night she sat up late altering the clothing, while Katie taught her everything that Mr. Haynes expected of his employees.

"We have to do something about your hair," Katie said carefully.

"What's wrong with my hair?" Caprice ran her hand over the shiny waves.

"It's too noticeable. If he had his way, we'd be invisible. He says he wants the service to be the only thing that leaves an impression. With your looks, you stand out in a crowd. To tell you the truth, he almost didn't hire you because of that."

"That's ridiculous!"

"Maybe so, but that's how he is. The only way I was able to convince him to hire you was to tell him you dye your hair. I said your real hair color is sort of drab."

"What!"

"He said he would give you a chance if you'd go back to your natural color."

"Katie, are you crazy? This *is* my natural color!"

"I know. So I bought this for you on my way home." She held out a box of ash-brown hair rinse.

"No!"

"It's not permanent. See? It says here that it washes out after five shampooings. I got this color because it was as far as I could get from red and still be light enough to look natural."

"I'm not going to do this!"

"Caprice, we need the money! Come on. What can it hurt?"

With a frown Caprice took the box and read the directions. "What if it doesn't wash out?"

"It does. I've used this brand myself. Remember when I decided to try life as a redhead?"

"All right," Caprice agreed with great reluctance, "but if I'm stuck with ash-brown hair, I'm going to get you but good!"

Half an hour later she emerged from the shower, wearing a robe and a towel wrapped around her head. Katie stood up expectantly as Caprice slowly pulled off the towel. Damp strands of mousy brown hair tumbled to her shoulders.

"Perfect!" Katie exclaimed. "Mr. Haynes will be so pleased!"

"It just tickles me to death that I've made Mr. Haynes's day," Caprice said listlessly.

"If you pull it back in a tight bun so it doesn't wave and if you don't wear any makeup, you'll be plain enough to be just about right."

"Thanks?"

"Come on now," Katie cajoled. "It's for a good cause."

"You're right about that. Heather is the only person in the world I'd do this for."

Katie's smile faded, and they both looked away. Each of them knew they couldn't hope to earn enough money by working at Sunny Day.

The next night they served at a retirement party. As Caprice wound her way through the crowd she heard snatches of gossip. She found herself filing away all the tidbits to tell Katie later. She was still surprised that no one bothered to hide even the most malicious tales from her. It was as if she were indeed invisible.

As she passed a huge gilt-framed mirror, Caprice caught her reflection and nearly dropped the tray of canapés. Her hair was slicked back in an unflattering bun and the color was still a shock to her. A good friend would have had trouble recognizing her. She had tailored the uniform, but the brown color wasn't right for her skin. She looked downright frumpy. With a sigh, she handed around the canapés and tried not to be resentful.

Fingers dripping with diamonds picked up the Russian caviar and pâté de foie gras as if such delicacies were mere potato chips. Elaborate watches set with sparkling jewels encircled fashionably skinny wrists. Bracelets that flashed and glittered graced plump wrists. Not a single woman in the room was without her diamonds or emeralds or rubies. When it occurred to Caprice that just a few of these baubles would save Heather's life, she set her lips firmly. Katie was right about the unfairness of life, Caprice thought pessimistically. What did these people care about a poor girl in the Heights? They were content to chatter on about who was sleeping with whom and who was vacationing where, and they didn't care at all about life itself.

She heard one woman tell another that Luke Banning had flown to Saint-Tropez for the week. Caprice wondered sourly how much that cost. At his sister's wedding he had mentioned a yacht; now it seemed he owned a private plane as well. She disliked herself for her bitterness, but she couldn't seem to control her feelings. Perhaps if she weren't surrounded by wealth, she could pretend no one had the amount of money Heather needed, but as it was, she felt like a starving child in a candy store.

She heard how Christine and Winston Norwood were installing a croquet lawn, and she wondered what that meant. As a child she and Katie had owned a battered croquet set and had spent hours batting a chipped ball through the rusty wickets. Caprice had had fun and had been pretty good at it, but she couldn't imagine an adult devoting an entire yard to the game.

When she went back for more hors d'oeuvres, she saw Katie coming out of the kitchen. "These people are crazy," Caprice whispered under her breath. "The Norwoods are turning their yard into a place to play croquet!"

Katie shrugged. "To each his own, I guess."

Caprice wasn't in a mood to be philosophical. She had spent the past week trying to get Heather's name before some organization with money for the transplant. Many of the people in the next room were either on the committees she had called, or they owned businesses that made philanthropic donations. Not one of them had been more than casually interested in Heather's plight.

As the chef put more caviar on her tray, Caprice contemplated how she would get the two-hundred thousand dollars. If only she could be accepted as one of them just long enough to plead Heather's case, there was a chance someone might make a donation. Unfortunately, she couldn't possibly enter into their elite circle.

Almost angrily Caprice took the loaded tray and headed back into the living room. Except for an accident of birth, Caprice would be eating fish eggs and goose liver instead of tuna and crackers. The idea brought a wry smile to her lips. She had never eaten caviar or pâté and never would; they smelled awful.

She could see Katie moving among the guests, her tray full of glasses. Her face was a mask, and Caprice couldn't tell if she were as resentful of all those diamonds and rubies as Caprice was. Knowing Katie, Caprice decided she probably wasn't. Katie had always been the sweet sister, whereas Caprice was the hellion. Katie accepted whatever life dished out, whether it was a philandering husband, poverty, or a desperately ill child. Caprice fought all the way.

She served a double-chinned matron who was lamenting the fact that June and Howard Walters would soon be leaving for a four-month vacation in the Far East, after which they would be in Turkey for two years while he supervised the construction of a nuclear power plant. Caprice managed, with great effort, to keep her face expressionless. She wondered if any of her purloined creations from Swayse's would be going abroad with June Walters.

As she began to pay closer attention to the faces, she noticed that even though some of the guests stayed only a short time, others arrived to take their place, and the room remained full. Caprice found herself wondering how they could all possibly know each other. Surely some were strangers to the others, but they all greeted one another with identical cool friendliness.

Intrigued, Caprice found herself listening even more closely to the bits of conversation. River Oaks had a dialect of its own; certain catch-words were tossed about liberally, primarily the names of resorts or the rich and famous, as well as their own. Even the accents and intonations sounded homogeneous. Name-dropping seemed to have become an indoor sport with these people. With her excellent memory for details, Caprice filed it all away, along with the cultured accent. Later, she thought, Katie and Heather would be amused to hear her imitations.

Chapter Three

Heather's medication reduced the fever that had been associated with a secondary infection, but it did nothing to improve her overall condition. The specialist, Dr. Eugene Granger, shook his head over the results of the second battery of tests.

"He said she isn't responding well to the medication," Katie reported to Caprice that night. "Heather's condition may be getting worse faster than he had expected."

Caprice finished laying out the stainless steel flatware before she asked the question she dreaded. "What did he suggest we should try next?"

"Dr. Granger stopped the medication for the infection, but increased the other to the maximum dosage.

He says we shouldn't get our hopes too high. She needs a transplant and nothing else will cure her.''

"Does she need it sooner than he first thought?"

Katie shook her head dismally as Caprice put the squash and chicken casserole on the table. "He said the sooner the better. It still might be a year before it's critical. It just depends on Heather."

They ate methodically. Heather, who usually liked the casserole, barely ate a bite. Caprice noticed her niece's skin had taken on a yellowish pallor. Her pale freckles stood out more clearly, and even the whites of her eyes seemed to have a sallow tint. The healthy luster was gone from her hair.

After Heather went into the living room to lie on the couch and watch TV, Katie washed the dishes while Caprice dried. "We've got to get that money!" Caprice said determinedly.

"How? Rob a bank?" Discouragement sounded dully in Katie's voice.

Caprice frowned at her. "I keep thinking of all those diamonds over in River Oaks."

"Great. We'll become cat burglars and wire the money to Dr. Granger from prison."

"I wasn't suggesting that. I just can't get them out of my mind."

"Do you expect one of those ladies to walk over and offer you her jewels to use in some worthy cause? Face facts, Cappy, life isn't like that."

The use of her childhood nickname hardened Caprice's determination to find some solution. "You were always there for me when we were children. In some ways you were more my mother than Mom was.''

Katie shrugged. "She was always at work, and you were the youngest. It's incredible, isn't it, that Mom and I both chose men who would desert us?'' She looked out at the fading sunset beyond the window. "I wonder where Jed is.''

"Don't worry about him—we have enough trouble right here.'' She put away the last plate and took the dripping baking dish from the plastic drainer. "You never let me down, Katie, and I won't let you down either.'' She was thoughtful as she wiped the casserole dish with the damp kitchen towel.

"It's not a matter of letting me down. It's a matter of things being out of our control. As sad as it is, we may have to accept it.''

"Don't you dare give up! You can't! Not with Heather's life at stake.''

Katie wheeled to face her sister, and Caprice saw the tears in her eyes. "Do you think I want to give up? That's my daughter in there!'' She pointed a trembling finger toward the living room. "I'm not giving up—I'm accepting something I can't change. Miracles don't happen! Not to people like us!''

"Yes, they do! And I'm going to arrange for one no matter what I have to do!''

"Oh? I can't wait to see you pull this off. What do you plan to do? Marry Luke Banning?'' Katie demanded sarcastically.

Caprice tilted her head thoughtfully. "He *is* the richest bachelor in town, isn't he? And we do know quite a bit about him.''

"Get serious," Katie snorted as she poured out the dish water into the wide sink and rinsed the plastic pan.

Caprice hung the dish towel on the metal rack and leaned back against the counter, her arms folded across her body. "That really would solve all our problems."

"Cappy, that's crazy. You could no more marry Luke Banning than you could fly to the moon!"

"No? Several people have flown to the moon, you know." Her green eyes sparkled with excitement. "It couldn't hurt to try, could it?"

"How are you even going to be able to talk to him? He's not likely to strike up a conversation with one of the caterer's waitresses. And besides, you know how Mr. Haynes would feel about that."

"Only if I speak to him while I'm working."

"That's the only time you can get within sight of him! You know how closely guarded their houses are. Do you plan to just walk up and ring his doorbell and propose?"

"Of course not. That would never work. But he's having a black-tie party on board his yacht at the end of the month. I think I'll go to it!"

"Just like that?" Katie said incredulously. "Just walk on board and nobody stop you? You're out of your mind."

"No, I'm not. I think I can pass as one of them. No one knows everybody at these parties."

"No, but the host must certainly know his guests."

"Not if one of the guests is a friend of one of his other guests. Or maybe a relative. Yes, a relative. That's better."

Katie stared at her sister.

"The Walters will be on their way to Japan and then to Turkey by the end of the month. I'm certain they would be invited, and I can pretend to be Mrs. Walters's cousin—or niece. I think her niece is better—a close kinship would be more believable. And it would explain why my last name isn't Walters."

"You'll be arrested!"

"It's not illegal to impersonate a Walters."

"You don't look anything like Mrs. Walters, and the Bannings are friends with them. You'll be discovered before you can get on board. Besides, you have to present an invitation at most of these parties. How will you get around that?"

"I'll figure that out later."

"I can't believe we're even discussing this. Forget the whole crazy idea."

"But it might work! You've said yourself that I can imitate that crowd to perfection."

"Sure you can here in my kitchen, but not in public! And this is a *black-tie* party! You don't have clothes like that!"

"You're right. That's a problem. But I do have a sewing machine and I didn't slave away at Swayse's for nothing! I could sew up one of my own designs."

"I feel as if Judy Garland and Mickey Rooney will come dancing through at any moment with plans to save the widow's farm with a performance in the barn.

You've come up with some wild notions before, but this one takes the cake.''

"We have a lot to lose and that calls for desperate measures." She ran her hand through her mousy brown hair. "Are you sure this rinse really does wash out?"

"I just hope you aren't thrown in jail. This isn't even logical, much less possible!"

"We won't know that until I try."

"Suppose this insane scheme works, and you convince him you're rich and get him to marry you. How are you going to tell him you need the money for your poor niece's operation? If he thinks you're rich, he'll wonder why you aren't using your own money. I don't know about all this. It's morally wrong!"

"No, it's not. When someone's as rich as Luke Banning, two hundred thousand dollars is nothing. He won't even miss it."

"What do you mean, 'won't even miss it?' You wouldn't take it from him without his knowing it. Would you?"

"There is no point in my telling him that I've married him for his money. I won't tell him anything until Heather gets her transplant. Then I'll agree to an uncontested divorce. He can go his way, and I'll go mine. Divorces are nothing to these rich playboy types."

"I don't like it."

"It's not illegal to marry for money. People do it all the time. It's not as if I plan to take more than I need. If it will make you feel better, we'll pay him back anonymously. Okay?"

Katie looked unconvinced, but she knew they were indeed forced to take desperate measures. Heather couldn't hold out for many months at the rate she was going downhill, and miracles really were rare in their section of town. "I guess if we pay him back, it's not so bad."

"Then it's settled."

"What do you plan to make this dress out of, Scarlett, the living room curtains?"

Caprice laughed and hugged Katie. "You leave that up to me. Your job is to coach me—voice, movements, gossip. Everything."

"I think I read Cinderella to you too often when you were little."

Again Caprice flashed her sister a dazzling smile. "From now on you're not to let me slip up in any way. Every word and each movement will have to seem natural." She thrust out her hips and held her head at a regal angle. "Shall we adjourn to the drawing room?"

Katie shook her head at Caprice's overemphatic gestures and her debutante slouch. "It'll never work."

Luke drove through Houston's rain-washed streets to the home of Philippa Hadley. He had known Philippa for several years and had a business connection with her father and one of her ex-husbands, but this date had been Christine's idea. Philippa lived in a redbrick colonial near Rice University in the South Hampton addition, where many of the homes rivaled those in River Oaks.

He parked beneath the live oaks that lined her drive and went up the shallow front steps to ring the bell. He was admitted by her maid and shown into the living room. Fifteen minutes later Luke glanced impatiently at his watch and sighed. Philippa was never on time, a habit he found extremely irritating, especially since she actually seemed to pride herself on the failing.

Ten minutes later she flowed into the room. Philippa always seemed to move as if she were mounted on wheels. She walked without a swing of her hips or bob of her head, her hands outstretched, palms down, to greet him. He kissed her cool cheek and listened to her usual apology for keeping him waiting, even though she knew their reservations were made and the Norwoods expecting them.

"Such beastly weather," she complained as they stepped out into the sultry dusk. "I keep threatening to move to a drier climate, but all my friends are here." She peered up at the dull sky. "We're to get more rain tonight, and you know how bad these streets are for flooding." She gave him a coy smile. "Wouldn't it be a shame if I were flooded out and had to spend the night at your place?"

Luke thought privately that it would indeed be a shame, since he already regretted having asked Philippa out. Gallantly he gave her a smile and made no comment.

At the Brownstone, an elegant four-star restaurant near the intersection of Westheimer and Kirby Drive, a uniformed valet parking attendant helped the couple out and whisked Luke's Maserati away. Luke held the door for Philippa to precede him into the restaurant's dim interior. The Brownstone had originally been a residence, the rooms of which had been converted into cozy dining areas. The entire restaurant was filled with expensive antiques that were available for purchase along with the meal. Overhead were classic chandeliers; beneath their feet were oriental rugs.

Christine and Winston were already seated at a table overlooking the pool. "So there you are," she said as the maître d' escorted them to the table. "We were beginning to think you two had made a side trip."

Philippa gave her response with a cryptic smile as if to intimate that Luke had suggested a pre-dinner dalliance, but that she had put him off. "It's so *heavy* in here," she remarked as she sat opposite Christine. "You'd have thought after the reopening that the ambiance would be less oppressive."

"It's all these antiques," Christine said with a nod. "It feels like a museum—or my mother's house." The women laughed as if Christine's statement had been of keen wit.

"Sorry to keep you waiting," Luke said to Winston. "Philippa has clocks all over her house, and she still can't be on time."

"Why, Luke," Philippa teased, "you haven't seen *all* of my house. Not yet, at least."

Christine arched her thin brows at her brother, but he ignored her. After they ordered, Winston began an excruciatingly boring account of the work being done to create his croquet lawn as Philippa commented on the absence of really good wine outside France. Luke gave every appearance of listening, but his mind wandered.

The two women were close friends, and Christine had insisted that a foursome was more fun than three at a table. Luke had nothing against Philippa, though he found her extremely shallow, so he had agreed. Thinking back, he now recalled he had asked her out more often than he had realized, and that Christine had all too frequently seated them together at her dinner parties. He was somewhat surprised that he had again fallen for his sister's matchmaking. He had let his guard down when Winston's sister was safely married to the count from Italy. Now Christine had another mate in mind for him. The pressure of Philippa's knee against his beneath the table confirmed it. Luke decided that after this evening he had better make it clear to Christine that he didn't want or need her help in the romance department.

On the surface, they might all have been no more than platonic friends—or couples married for years, Philippa and Christine chatted about a fur they had seen in Neiman-Marcus and Winston talked on about a proposed merger between two steel companies.

After they ate their chateaubriand, Winston ordered a slice of Mile High pie, a Brownstone speciality, for each of them. When the flaming dessert was served, Philippa gasped and gushed that it was almost worth the wait just to look at it. Christine merely pushed hers aside with a comment about watching her weight. Winston attacked the layers of ice cream with gusto.

All the while, Luke watched them as if they were strangers. People had always fascinated him, including those he knew well.

"Would you look at that?" Philippa said accusingly as the first fat drops of rain spattered into the pool outside the window. "Rain!"

"Not again!" Christine's hand automatically touched her perfectly coiffed hair. "I thought we were through for today at least."

With a heavy-lidded look that was supposed to be seductive, Philippa raised her empty wine glass to signal the waiter and pressed her knee more firmly against Luke's. "I wouldn't be surprised if my street is flooded within minutes."

"At this rate Houston will soon look like Venice," Winston predicted gloomily. "With our present rate of subsidence . . ."

Luke only half-listened. He rather enjoyed rain, although Houston did get more than its share and flooding was always a problem. "Venice is nice in the springtime," he said almost absently.

"Well, what place isn't?" Philippa laughed a bit too loudly. She had had several glasses of wine, and she wasn't an accomplished drinker. "I'd love to see Venice with you," she added in what she seemed to think was an undertone.

"I think I had better see you home now," Luke said with an indulgent smile.

"Don't be in such a rush," Philippa said as she motioned for the waiter. "Bring me a grasshopper."

"Crème de menthe on top of wine?" Christine said. "You shouldn't do that."

"Of course I should. I do it all the time."

"Bring us the check, please," Luke said to the waiter.

"*And* a grasshopper. To go," she added with a giggle.

"You're going to hate yourself in the morning," Christine warned.

"I doubt it will take that long," Luke said. "We'll have some coffee."

"And don't forget my grasshopper," Philippa warned playfully.

Luke shrugged and nodded in dismissal to the waiter. "You're making a big mistake, Philippa."

"Nonsense. After dinner drinks just make me more cuddly." She leaned toward him and narrowly missed putting her elbow in the butter.

"What's wrong with you?" Christine hissed. "You never get drunk in public!"

"I'm not drunk now." Philippa's words slurred slightly. "I only had a little vodka before I left the house and a glass of wine with my meal."

Luke groaned. "And you plan to have a grasshopper? I think we should leave now."

Christine glared at her friend. "I think you're right, Luke."

Before they could find the waiter, he appeared with the coffee and a pale green drink. As Luke signed the check, Philippa took a large swallow. Instantly she paled and her eyes grew round. "Christine?" she gasped weakly.

"Come with me." Christine took her arm and led her toward the women's room.

Winston shook his head sagely. "I don't know why she drinks like that. None of the Hadleys can hold his liquor."

Luke frowned. He hated an unpleasant scene, especially a public one. He didn't need to look around to know their table had become something of a spectacle. "I should have watched her more carefully."

"Philippa's a big girl," Winston said. "You aren't her guardian."

"If it were up to Christine, I would be. Tell her to lay off the matchmaking, will you?"

"I'll tell her, but it won't do any good. You know Christine. She wants to see you happily married."

"Philippa Hadley isn't the one."

"I can see your point."

After several long minutes, the women rejoined them. Christine looked miffed and Philippa contrite. She was still unsteady on her feet, and as they waited for Luke's Maserati and Winston's Lincoln, Luke put his arm around Philippa's waist to steady her. She laid her head on his broad shoulder, leaving a smudge of makeup on his lapel. Luke's accusing eyes met his sister's over Philippa's head. Christine made a helpless gesture that said this wasn't her fault. Luke knew it wasn't, but he still blamed her, especially when Philippa put her arms around him and rose on tiptoe to make a graphic suggestion as to how they could spend the rest of the evening.

Luke all but shoved her into the car and glared at his sister as he hurried around to the driver's side. If he made good time he could deposit Philippa at her house and get home before the streets became impassable.

* * *

Three days later Luke went to Christine's house for one of her small cocktail parties. She had assured him that Philippa Hadley wasn't invited, but nevertheless Luke was relieved and his spirits lifted when he saw that Philippa's car wasn't in the drive. Since the disastrous evening at the Brownstone, Philippa had called him several times with apologies and invitations. Luke graciously accepted the former and declined the latter, but Philippa told him over and over again that she didn't give up easily.

He went into Christine's rose-and-white living room and his eyes narrowed as he realized there was only one other guest. He spoke to his sister and brother-in-law, then smiled warily at the woman. "Hello, Luana, I haven't seen you for a while."

"I've been in Hawaii. Oahu, to be exact. Waikiki. It's terribly touristy, but then I *was* a tourist." Her staccato burst of laughter resembled the sound of a barking seal.

Luke looked sideways at Christine, who handed him a cool drink, but wouldn't meet his eyes. "Luana tells me she's hired the same decorator I did. Perhaps you should have him out to redo your house as well."

"No, thanks, I like my house just as it is." He turned to Winston. "How are you doing these days?"

"Fine, fine. The workmen have started laying the PVC pipe for the drainage system on my croquet lawn."

"It seems to be taking a long time."

"You can't rush these things. Not if you're going to do it right." Winston's expression was set in firm lines of concern.

"I adore croquet," Luana said with a heartfelt sigh.

Luke maneuvered his sister away on the pretext of examining a new painting she had commissioned. "What are you doing to me?" he muttered under his breath. "And why?"

"It's all for your own good."

He gave her a frown and she added, "Okay, so Philippa was a mistake. I forgot about her drinking problem. And maybe Winston's sister might not have been quite right either, but Luana Beaufort is as nice as they come."

"Back off, Christine. I don't need any help. I don't want a wife."

"Of course you do. You're a romantic, and your kind *needs* a good marriage."

"I don't want one," he repeated. "And I don't want Luana Beaufort, either."

"You're too damned hard to please," Christine whispered acidly. "Just give her a chance." She whirled back to join the others. "Luke says he likes the painting, Winston. I knew he would."

"Who wouldn't?" Luana commented with a breathy sigh. "I love seascapes."

"He must have found a sale on blue paint," Luke observed.

"I love blue," Luana said.

The conversation swung to yachts, which Luana professed to adore, and to deep sea fishing, which

Luana had never tried but which she was sure she would love if she had.

"I prefer floating to fishing," Luke said. "I never know what to do with a fish as big as I am. I always throw them back."

"I enjoy traveling by yacht," Luana agreed promptly.

Luke raised his eyebrows at his sister. "Speaking of yachts, are you all coming to my party at the end of the month?"

"I wouldn't miss it," Luana gushed. "I always enjoy parties so much." She put down the drink she had scarcely sipped. "Goodness this is good, but I'm not much of a drinker."

Christine smiled triumphantly at Luke. "Winston and I will be there. Have you arranged for a caterer?"

"Ralph Slayton takes care of all those details for me. You know I don't like planning parties."

"I wish I had a manager like Ralph," Winston said enviously. "He's like a business partner and a mother all rolled into one."

Luke laughed. "He takes better care of me than is necessary at times."

"A wife usually does those things. Makes party arrangements, I mean," Luana said.

"I don't have a wife, so I make do with Ralph."

"I know," she said silkily. "When I was married I used to just love doing things like that for my husband. Little dinner parties and soirées, and things." She sighed in domestic remembrance.

"The best part about Ralph is that he doesn't care if I stay out late, and he never expects a new wardrobe or gets mad if I forget his birthday," Luke said with determined joviality. "I think I'll stick with him."

Again Luana's barking laugh sounded. "I just love your sense of humor, Luke. Truly I do!"

As Luana hung on Winston's explanation of why a croquet lawn's soil had to be sterilized, Christine cornered Luke. "She's a very nice person, and she is certainly easy to please," she said defensively before Luke could speak.

"Loving everything is just as phony as hating everything like Philippa does. Neither of them says what she really thinks."

"Well, what's so bad about that? At least she's pleasant to be around."

"She's too plastic. And too transparent. I'll bet she could quote the price of every wedding ring in the Galleria."

"Domesticity isn't much of a fault. What are you looking for in a woman, for goodness' sake?"

He sighed. "I don't know. Every woman I know is so blasted predictable. I don't think anyone has surprised me—*really* surprised me—in years."

"You're rather young to be so jaded," his sister complained. "I think you're just being difficult."

"Then give up and leave me alone," he retorted.

"I'll see you happily married if it kills you!" Christine jerked up her chin and turned to join the others.

Luke laughed softly. When she wasn't being such a pain in the neck, Christine was interesting to be around. Her motives were good, even if she sometimes was rather pompous and full of her own importance.

Chapter Four

Caprice began her preparations early in the afternoon, shampooing her hair over and over until all the mousy tint went down the drain, leaving behind a natural pale-red sheen. Ritualistically, she smoothed moisturizing cream over her face, neck, arms, and legs, rubbing it into her silky skin. Next she blew her hair dry and brushed it into gleaming waves before pinning a classical Grecian braid on top of her head.

Makeup came next, and she took care to apply it with precision. First, a translucent face powder, then pale blush for a hint of color across her cheeks. Next she brushed brown eye shadow on her upper lids, and a muted green shade just above her eyelashes, which she accentuated with mascara. With satisfaction, she noted that her green eyes appeared more vivid and se-

ductive than before. The finishing touch was the deep
coral lipstick that left her lips looking moist, as though
she had just licked them with the tip of her tongue.

Carefully she put on her panties and smoothed on
her pantyhose, then stepped into her dress. The can-
dlelight white fabric floated about her like a night
breeze, now clinging to her curves, now swinging free.
Its Grecian lines were deceptively simple, yet extremely elegant. Because she owned no jewels, she had
designed a draped neckline that made jewelry super-
fluous. She fastened the thin straps of her white high-
heeled sandals and turned to look at herself in the
mirror.

Caprice was amazed at her reflection. This was a
person she had never seen before. She looked as if she
had been born and raised in the palatial splendor of
River Oaks. Her bedroom, with its faded bedspread
and curtains seemed an incongruous setting for her
elegance.

She put her car keys, driver's license, and lipstick in
the white beaded bag she had bought in a secondhand
shop near River Oaks. Suddenly she was afraid—not
only that her bizarre scheme might fail, but also that
it might succeed. She didn't know this man from
Adam and here she was, planning to marry him!

Curiously, this had never occurred to her. Luke
Banning had figured so prominently in her day-
dreams that she had never considered anyone else. He
might be thoroughly boorish, or some kind of a per-
vert! Even more likely, she could very well be wasting
a lot of time and effort on a plan that would never
work.

Caprice eased herself down on the edge of her bed and stared at the stranger in the mirror. This was a ridiculous idea! Even assuming she could attract him for one evening, how could she possibly pull off this masquerade all the way to the altar? And if she did, how could she fool him day in and day out until she had the money Heather needed? Was this fraud? She wasn't so sure anymore.

She jumped when Katie knocked on her bedroom door. "It's eight o'clock. Aren't you dressed yet?"

Caprice stood up and lifted her chin. She couldn't let Katie and Heather down. A life depended on this.

She opened the door and stepped into the living room. By Katie's expression and Heather's giggle, she knew she wasn't wrong. She did look entirely different. Moving as if charm schools were her second home, Caprice breezed to the center of the room and whirled around for effect.

"You're gorgeous!" Katie exclaimed. "I wouldn't guess it was you if I didn't know better."

Caprice laughed. "You have quite a way with words. Luckily I know what you meant by that."

"You look like a princess in my fairy tale book," Heather spoke up enthusiastically.

"Now there's a compliment to take with me," Caprice responded with another smile. To Katie she said, "What do you really think? Can I pull this off?"

"There's no doubt in my mind."

"I wish there weren't any in mine."

"Look at it this way—if we could get the money any other way, if they would give us what we need, we wouldn't have to do this. They practically owe it to us. Goodness knows they can afford it.''

A slight frown puckered Caprice's forehead as she told them goodbye and went out to her rusting Pontiac. Katie had sounded so harsh in her judgment of these people. They weren't to blame for Heather's illness. The closer she got to the yacht basin, the more doubts assailed her. Upon entering Galveston, she wanted to turn around and go home.

She parked in the area blocked off for the hired help in the marina dining room, where her Pontiac's dented fender and faded red paint wouldn't stand out. For a moment she sat there, perfectly still, her hands clutching the steering wheel. Of all the farfetched ideas she had ever come up with, this was the most unlikely of them all. But she had come too far now to back out.

Before she could run away, she got out of the car and hurried around to the front of the marina. Soft lanterns lit her way along the walk to the dock. Rows of yachts, most of them dark and deserted, lined either side. She had no trouble finding the *Idlewild*. It was by far the largest boat in the marina and the only one with a party on its decks.

The *Idlewild* loomed like a white phantasm in the inky water. The crowded decks were illuminated with subtle lights and inside the two saloons she could see people moving about and laughing over their drinks. Caprice boarded beside a gleaming ship's bell inscribed with *Idlewild*. As she stepped onto the bleached wood of the foredeck, a man wearing a white nautical uniform met her and politely held out his hand for her invitation.

This was the moment of truth. Caprice gestured airily with her fingers and gave him her most bedazzling smile. "I never bother carrying around those things. Obviously I was invited or I wouldn't have known to come." She breezed past him and before he could stop her, she waved at the nearest couple. "Hello, Sam, Maureen. My goodness, but I adore that dress, Maureen. Did Swayse's do it for you?" She left the crewman staring after her as she insinuated herself between the two guests.

The woman caught herself gaping at Caprice, who was obviously waiting for her answer. "Why, yes, this is a Swayse's original."

Her husband was more blunt. "Excuse me, but have we met?"

"Well, of course," Caprice said with just the right touch of reproof. "At Christine's wedding reception. Don't you remember me?"

"Yes, yes," Sam said quickly to hide the fact he didn't remember her at all. "How are you?"

"Fine, thank you." She looked around as if to see which of her close friends might be there. "What a pity Aunt June and Uncle Howard couldn't make it. I guess they're in Japan by now."

Maureen's face broke into an excited smile. "Now I know who you are. You mean June and Howard Walters!" She cast a look at her husband as if to reprimand him for not helping her place the young woman. "This is Howard's . . . niece."

"No, no, I'm from Aunt June's side of the family. My grandmother and hers were sisters. Caprice Dolan is my name."

"That's right," Maureen gushed in relief. "How foolish of me not to remember."

"It's so nice to see you again. Won't you excuse me? I see a friend over there I must speak to." Caprice melted into the crowd. She knew enough people from Swayse's and the parties to greet a passable number of the guests by name. In no time she had complete confidence that this would work after all.

Luke mixed with his guests, spending time with each group. He had noticed a strange woman with hair like pale fire and a white gown, but she always seemed to be across the room or going from one deck to the other. He wasn't particularly surprised to see someone that he hadn't expressly invited. Out of a hundred guests there were several who had brought a date. He was, however, taken aback that he had never seen her before. He was positive he would have remembered hair that color, especially coupled with such a radiant smile. He saw her edging away from the press of the crowd, a drink in her hand. He excused himself from his current conversation and followed her, not taking his eyes from her slender figure lest he lose her again.

Caprice made her way to the rail for a breath of fresh air. Crowds often bothered her, and the noisy, smoke-filled rooms were stifling. So far she hadn't even caught a glimpse of Luke Banning and the evening was ticking away. She had never considered the possibility of not being able to speak to him at the party. Taking a sip of her vodka and tonic, she looked out at the black waters of the bay. The full moon cast a golden path over the rippling waters, its brilliance hiding the stars in the sooty sky. She had to go back inside and find Luke Banning—she couldn't come this far and fail.

She turned and almost ran into his broad chest. Her eyes shot up to meet his, and for a terrible moment she thought he was going to denounce her as a party crasher.

Luke looked down into the sea-green depths of her eyes and found his senses reeling. Her coral lips parted to show even white teeth, and he wondered what her lips would feel like beneath his own. She was a bit taller than average, but was still considerably shorter than he. Her body was slender, yet she looked more athletic than gaunt. To his amazement, he detected a spark of fear in her eyes. Shyness, he assumed. To put her at her ease, he smiled. "Hello," he said softly.

"Hello." Caprice was too stunned to say more. His complete attention was unnerving. The intense silver eyes seemed to be reading her innermost thoughts.

"My name is Luke Banning. Welcome to the *Idlewild*."

"Thank you." Suddenly she remembered what she was there to do and said, "I'm Caprice Dolan, June Walters's niece."

"Oh? I wasn't aware she had a niece."

Caprice shrugged. "I haven't lived in Houston long. I guess she just never saw any reason to mention me."

He looked unconvinced, so she hastily changed the subject. "I love your yacht. Have you had it long?"

"It was finished several months ago. Would you like a tour?"

When she smiled at him, her face glowed with a beauty that made his breath catch in his throat. "I'd like that."

Luke put his hand on her elbow and guided her through the crowd to the steps. When they reached the top, he said, "This is the helicopter pad. I sent it ashore tonight to make room for dancing." He guided her around the small band and down a stairway to the enclosed solarium.

Caprice admired a rugged bronze statue of an old man in a boat. "How beautiful!"

"It's called *The Old Man and the Sea*. A friend of mine commissioned it for me as a gift."

She crossed the room for a better look at a portrait of an eighteenth-century nobleman, obviously hung there in counterpoint to the modern decor. She raised her eyebrows questioningly. "An ancestor?"

"No, a sense of humor. This is the seventh Earl of Wyndfell. I made his acquaintance at an estate sale in London, and thought he would lend the boat some class."

"He does that without a doubt. In fact," she said with a laugh, "he doesn't look as if he ever had a doubt in his life."

"That's what drew me to him." Luke grinned down at her. "You'd be surprised how many people have assured me there's a strong family resemblance between my 'ancestor' and myself."

"Not really," she said with a laugh.

"It's the sort of thing most people would want to hear, I guess." He led her down another short flight of steps to the main saloon where most of the guests were gathered. He spoke genially to several people as they crossed the room. As in the solarium, the furniture was overstuffed to inviting plumpness, ranging in hues from sky blue to a pale blue-green. The ceiling, as in all the rooms below deck, was thickly padded in white leather. The carpet was the color of moss.

"I've never seen anything so beautiful," she said in all honesty. She went to a painting of an ancient sailing ship, its tattered sail unfurled, emerging from a fog bank.

"*The Flying Dutchman*," he explained. "I got the idea from the charts used to spot enemy ships at sea. If any of my crew happen to see the *Flying Dutchman*, I want them to be able to identify her."

Caprice laughed with delight. "You aren't anything like I had imagined you!"

"No? Then we really haven't met before?"

She turned away. "What's down this way?"

He smiled and gestured for her to enter the short hall. "These are the guest staterooms," he said, opening one of the teakwood doors. The cozy room had been decorated in the same colors and style as the solarium and adjoining saloon.

Caprice was intrigued. She had lived in Houston all her life and had been to Galveston countless times, but she had never been on a yacht, or even near one. At the end of the short hall he opened another door to show her a smaller and more intimate saloon that was unoccupied. The block paneling of bird's-eye maple seemed to ripple like golden honey. The puffy chairs were covered in white ducking, and there were built-in bookshelves behind latticed doors.

Luke watched her with great interest. She seemed to be examining everything as though she had never been on a yacht before. Naturally that was ridiculous, because June and Howard Walters had a 58-foot Hatteras that was their pride and joy.

"I didn't expect it to be so big!" she marveled as she opened yet another door. "Oh! It's your bedroom!" She tried to shut the door, but he moved up close behind her and pushed it further open.

"You may as well see it all," he said as he looked down into her eyes. She was so close he could smell her faint perfume and see the turquoise flecks in her eyes. That must be why they were such a vivid color, he surmised. Most green eyes had gold in them, not blue. At first he had thought she was wearing tinted contact lenses.

She abruptly turned away and stepped into the room as if his nearness was unsettling. Luke followed her. "I had the walls in here covered with foam and fabric in addition to other soundproofing techniques that the interior designer used. This cabin is the closest one to the engine room, but the roar of the engines is virtually unnoticeable."

As in the other rooms, the ceiling was covered in soft rolls of white leather, but in contrast to the well-lit saloon, the lighting here was warm and intimate. She touched the pale blue-green walls; they were quite soft. The room was dominated at one end by a king-sized bed with an emerald green spread and at the other by a built-in couch below a wide window.

"It overlooks the wake," he went on. "I think it's as important to see where I've been as where I'm

going. When we pull out into the Gulf, sea gulls follow behind the yacht to fish. It's a pretty sight.''

She started to walk past him to rejoin the others, but
he caught her wrist, firmly but not threateningly.
''Let's not go back just yet.''

Her startlingly green eyes met his. ''But you're the
host.''

''Exactly. And as such I should have some privileges.''

Caprice didn't know quite what to say. She had
heard of the decadent parties thrown by the rich, but
she hadn't really believed the stories. At least not entirely. She liked this man a lot more than she had
expected. Somehow it had never occurred to her that
Luke Banning might have a sense of humor that would
include something as off-the-wall as installing the
portrait of a fake ancestor in his yacht. It was almost
as if he laughed at his own wealth. All things considered, though, she had no intention of doing something foolish just because he fascinated her. With her
coolest reserve, she said, ''I don't think—''

''Did you see this painting?'' he asked, unexpectedly interrupting her refusal with a sudden change of
subject. ''It's the only one on board that I take seriously.''

When Caprice stepped toward the canvas for a better look, her lips parted in surprise. The subjects were
a mermaid surrounded by a cape of floating jade hair
and her lover, whose matching pale green body was
floating close to her. The mermaid's expression was
that of pure love. The intensely emotional theme
evoked a very sensual mood. The couple was ob-

viously in love. "I've never seen anything like this. It's as if they're alive."

"I know. Technically I guess it's not the artist's best work, but I like it. Besides, Christine thinks it's nouveau riche, and I like to get her ire up. Do you know Christine?" he asked unexpectedly.

"No," Caprice said before she thought. Then more cautiously, she added, "Of course I've met her, but we aren't close."

"I thought not. She wouldn't have missed inviting you over to one of her cocktail parties." What a pity, he thought. This woman was far more interesting than Luana Beaufort and Philippa Hadley combined.

"I'd like to get to know her better," Caprice said smoothly. "Will she be here tonight?"

"Yes, she and Winston were delayed, but they're coming later." He surveyed her as frankly as if she were a fascinating work of art. "You haven't lived here in Houston for long?"

"No, I moved here only a few months ago."

"Why haven't I seen you at the Walters's or at any of the parties or the Country Club?"

"To tell you the truth, Aunt Jane and I aren't terribly close. As for the parties, I guess you must have overlooked me."

"Not a chance." His unsettling eyes searched hers. "If you were in the room, I would have seen you."

"That's where you're wrong. I was at Christine's wedding reception, and you looked straight through me."

His brow furrowed slightly. He was absolutely certain he had never seen her before.

"You said you were late because you ran into bad weather and that the *Idlewild* is no match for a tropical storm."

"I remember saying that."

She smiled and turned away to stroll over to the couch and sit down. Now she had the upper hand. Her weakest point was suddenly her strongest one—he was intrigued by her mysteriousness. "You couldn't make it to the Overmeyer party because you were in Saint-Tropez. Did you have a good time?"

He sat beside her on the couch and put his arm along the cushioned back. "You seem to know me much better than I know you."

His deep voice was velvety in the quietness of the room, and she could feel the heat from his hand less than an inch from her neck. Her skin prickled with the desire to have him touch her, even briefly. "It would seem that way, wouldn't it?"

"And you knew I was in Saint-Tropez," he mused aloud. "To answer your question, the trip was informative. I wasn't there for pleasure this time."

She wondered what that meant, but she smiled as if she knew exactly what he was talking about. "We should get back to the others," she suggested.

As she had hoped, he shook his head. "There's no rush. No one will miss us in that crush." He smiled and added, "I'm not very fond of crowds."

"You aren't?" This really surprised her. Caprice thought all the Bannings lived to party.

"Christine dotes on crowds, the bigger the better. So do my parents. As for myself, I usually have two parties a year, and I invite everyone I can think of to relieve my social obligations. Other than that, I live a relatively quiet life.''

Caprice looked around the yacht's master bedroom. This was what he considered quiet living? He would probably consider the two hundred thousand she needed as mere petty cash. Her resolve strengthened. "I'm a rather quiet person myself."

"I've noticed that. It's rare for me to do all the talking. Usually it's the other way around. Where did you say you moved here from?''

"I didn't." She leaned comfortably into the curved corner of the couch. "Tell me about the *Idlewild*. It fascinates me."

For a moment he studied her as if he hadn't heard her. Then he said, "She's a 155-foot yacht, weighs four hundred and seventy tons, and is powered by twin nine-hundred-horsepower diesel engines. She cruises at fourteen knots and has a permanent crew of fourteen."

"One for each knot," she said with amusement. "That's nice."

"There were thirteen in my crew, but Christine insisted that was pushing my luck too far. The captain's younger brother was laid off from a luxury liner just when we were christening the *Idlewild*, so I gave him a job. That made Captain Tolliver and his brother happy, and I got a terrific cook into the bargain."

"That must have pleased your sister, too."

"Not especially. She wanted me to fire one, not hire an extra. She thinks I'm being extravagant." He grinned, and she felt lost in his hypnotic gaze.

"Are you? Extravagant, I mean."

"Probably."

She forced herself to look away. "Have they finished their croquet lawn?"

"So you know about that, too? No, they haven't. Winston keeps making 'improvements' in the design. It's the best toy he's ever had."

Caprice had heard a hint about the price of this 'toy,' and her eyes hardened as she thought of the number of sick children who could have received life-giving medical care for the cost of the croquet lawn.

"Did I say something wrong?"

She forced a smile back to her face. "Of course not. I was just thinking that if someone walked in, we would seem to be in a rather compromising situation."

"No one will walk in."

"Why not?"

"I locked the door."

"What! Why did you do that?"

"So no one would walk in." He took her hand in his. "No rings. No husband?"

"No. No husband." The unexpected caress made her heart flutter like a frightened butterfly. She knew she should pull away, but she couldn't have moved if the yacht were on fire.

"In fact, you're wearing no jewelry at all. Not even earrings."

She tilted her head to one side and gave him an enigmatic smile. "I didn't feel like wearing any tonight."

"Most women wouldn't go as far as the nearest shopping mall without jewelry of some sort. I find that intriguing. You aren't like anyone I've ever met before.''

''That's right,'' she said with a broad smile. ''I'm not.''

''Are you engaged? Divorced? Tell me about yourself.''

''I'm not engaged, and I've never been married.''

''Why not? It can't be because no one ever proposed.''

''As corny as it may sound, I never found anyone I would give up my freedom for.''

''Marriage doesn't have to mean a loss of freedom.''

''No? That hasn't been my observation.''

''It can mean freedom of a different sort. One involving two people instead of just one.''

Her breath caught in her throat. When he stroked her hand and looked at her in that soul-searching way, she felt herself go hot in the strangest places. She couldn't care for him! She was only there to get the money for Heather's operation. Nothing else. But his hands were warm and firm, and his eyes compelled her to trust in him. If he were anyone but Luke Banning, Caprice would fall in love with him before the night was over. She knew it all the way down to her bones.

To break the spell, she gave a short laugh. ''Sometimes it means freedom for one—like my brother-in-law, for instance.'' At once she could have bitten her tongue.

Instead of asking the brother-in-law's name, as she was afraid he would, Luke said, ''That's not a marriage. When two people are really married—whether they have a legal ceremony or not—they don't want to stray."

"You seem to be an expert on marriage," she whispered.

"I am. I saw firsthand all the wrong things to do. If I can find someone the exact opposite of my ex-wife, I'll be a happy man."

"Oh? And what sort of woman would that be?" she asked with real interest.

"An honest one. A woman I could trust to be as faithful as I am."

Silence overwhelmed the room. Caprice knew he was about to kiss her, and she was torn between wanting him to and being afraid that he would. She liked him—she liked him too much. She wasn't the honest and true woman he was looking for, and guilt made her turn away.

Luke caught her chin and cradled it for a moment in his palm as if he were memorizing her face down to the most minute detail. Then he slowly lowered his head and kissed her. At first his lips were gentle upon hers, then as the kiss deepened, he gathered her into his embrace, and Caprice slipped her arms around him. His hair was thick and soft beneath her fingers and his shoulders broad under his coat. She felt the leashed strength of his mounting passion and answered it with a matching ardor of her own.

She had been kissed many times, but never like this. Luke knew exactly how to please her and how to draw out her emotions to the full. The room seemed to whirl as she gave herself more eagerly to him and he held back nothing of himself. At once she realized that along with his sensitivity and tenderness, he was surprisingly vulnerable.

Filled with disgust at herself as she remembered what she had come here to do, Caprice pulled back and tried to rise from the couch. Luke caught her and gazed deep into her eyes. "Why did you pull away?" he implored in a tone that was barely more audible than a whispered endearment.

Caprice didn't know how to answer him. Certainly she couldn't tell him the truth. "I'm...I'm not that sort of a woman," she stammered inanely.

He looked at her as if he couldn't believe she had actually said that. He began to chuckle, softly at first, then laughed outright, the timbre of his voice deep and hearty.

Caprice immediately realized the ridiculousness of her words and laughed despite herself. Every time they almost stopped laughing, their eyes would meet and they would start again. "Well, I'm not," she was finally able to say in protest.

"Can I see you tomorrow night?" he asked unexpectedly.

"Tomorrow?"

"We could go out for dinner and maybe go dancing at the Country Club. Where do you live?"

"No! I mean, I'm not sure I'm going to be free tomorrow evening. Could I call you?"

His amused eyes met hers. In addition to all her other attributes, she wasn't trying to move in too fast as Luana did or too possessively as Philippa had. He gave her his card and wrote his home phone number on the back. "Don't lose it. It's unlisted."

She smiled. "I won't lose it."

Before he could stop her, she stood and went to the door. "I have to go now."

"So soon? We're only now getting to know each other."

"I know," she replied with her mysterious smile.

Luke didn't know what to say. He wasn't at all accustomed to having to persuade a woman to stay. "You'll call me?"

"You'll be hearing from me." She slid out the door and closed it behind her, then sought the safety of the crowd before she could change her mind and run into his arms.

"Wait!" Luke exclaimed. "You didn't give me your number." He hurried to the door, but the room beyond was empty. When he went into the main saloon, he was met by a wall of noisy people, and Caprice was nowhere in sight. He searched for her, but she had disappeared like sea fog. With a puzzled expression, Luke leaned on the yacht's railing and gazed out into the night.

Chapter Five

It's a shame you missed the party Saturday," Luke said as his financial manager, Ralph Slayton, rummaged through his bulging briefcase.

"One of us had to work," Ralph said dryly as he pulled out several stapled pages.

"Not all the time. Don't you ever take time off?"

"Not if I can help it." Ralph peered at the papers through his thick, horn-rimmed glasses. "I like to work." He smiled, and his features softened, but only slightly.

"You were born an adult. On the tennis court, I can see you calculating the angle of the ball's path and the height of the net to the exact centimeter."

"I must be doing it right; you'll notice I bested you yesterday."

"A lucky fluke," Luke grinned. "Meet me on center court this afternoon, and I'll prove it."

"Nope, I have a dozen things to do. So do you. You're to go downtown and sign those gas lease papers."

"Can't they mail them to me like they always do?"

"While you're down there, you have an appointment with a Mr. Ehud ben Yaron about that Middle Eastern pipeline."

"I forgot all about that!"

"That's why you hired me." Again, Ralph smiled.

Luke wondered how such opposites as themselves had managed to establish a friendship. Ralph had a computer for a brain, never dated at all, and had virtually no sense of humor. On the other hand, he was loyal to a fault, never forgot appointments, and would track down the most obscure detail to make his books balance or his files complete.

The thought of missed appointments brought a frown to Luke's face. Caprice Dolan had not called as she had said she would. "Do you know someone named Dolan who recently moved here? Caprice is her first name. She's the niece of June Walters."

"Dolan, Dolan, Caprice Dolan. June Walters. Nope, can't say as I've ever heard of her. Why do you ask?"

"I met her at my party. The Walters have gone out of town, as you know, and she evidently used their invitation to get on board."

"What do you mean 'evidently?' "

"That's the only way she could have walked past my crewman. You should see her, Ralph. Eyes so green they reminded me of leaves, and hair that's neither red nor pale gold, but some shade in between.''

"She sounds very colorful. Sign these papers here where I put the X." He leaned forward to point his ascetically thin finger toward the line.

"You wouldn't be so phlegmatic if you'd seen her. I never saw such a beautiful woman in my life. And her laugh! It sounded like bubbling water.''

"She must be truly amazing," Ralph responded in a uninterested voice.

As Luke studied his friend for a moment, he wondered for perhaps the millionth time if Ralph were not attracted to women or just too work-oriented to be interested. "She's more than just amazing. I can't stop thinking about her. Do you know what she did? She stood me up!''

"No wonder you can't get her out of your mind. That's probably never happened to you before." He raised his head and the overhead light revealed the prematurely bald spot where his black hair didn't quite cover his crown. Ralph's skin had a milky-blue cast that made his hair seem extraordinarily dark, and his cheeks were always bluish with the faint hint of his shaved beard. "I guess she didn't exactly stand me up," Luke amended. "I asked her out, and she said she would call and tell me yes or no.''

"She had to ask permission? How old is she exactly?''

"No, no, nothing like that. I guess she didn't know if she was free or not. Anyway, she didn't call. Why do you suppose she didn't?''

"Maybe she wasn't as taken with you as you were with her. Maybe she simply lost your number. Why don't you call her and ask?"

"That's why I was asking if you know her. There's no Caprice Dolan or C. Dolan listed in the book, and I didn't think to get her phone number."

"Never heard of her. When you talk to Yaron, hold firm on our previous stand. I've already worked out the details, but he may try to sway you on percentages."

"I can handle that, but why do you suppose Caprice didn't call?"

"Perhaps she's...capricious?" Ralph looked at Luke and smiled again.

"Ralph, you astound me. Can it be that you're developing a sense of humor?"

"I shouldn't think so." Ralph snapped his briefcase shut. "Don't be late for the appointment. I've heard Yaron is a real stickler for punctuality."

"Don't let this shake you up, but I think Caprice Dolan may be the woman I've been searching for."

Ralph studied him through his bifocals. "Find out her phone number before you propose." He swung the heavy briefcase off the table and nodded a farewell to Luke. "Are we still on for tennis next Wednesday?"

"Sure thing. I plan to trounce you."

"We'll see. I wouldn't count on it, though." Ralph waved and let himself out.

Luke sauntered across the thick blue carpet of his business manager's office and gazed out the window. Somewhere out there Caprice Dolan was going about her everyday life, probably not even thinking about their meeting and the kiss that had changed his existence.

Caprice hadn't called Luke for the simple reason that she had nothing to wear on a date. In view of her success at the party, Katie insisted that she buy more material, as well as second-hand clothing from the resale shop, and make herself a wardrobe. Bait, as Katie termed it.

Now that she had her foot in the door of River Oaks, Caprice was hesitating. She liked Luke Banning, liked his vulnerability, something that she had never expected. Heather, however, was an implacable motivation. Caprice couldn't afford to be squeamish about marrying into the Banning fortune, and she couldn't even tell Katie of her reticence, because Katie would certainly think she had lost her mind. Anyone in her right mind would jump at the chance to marry a handsome millionaire.

After five days, Caprice had enough clothes to start dating Luke, but she put off calling him until Katie came home from work. She needed her sister's moral support. Even then she was reluctant to dial his number. Since she hadn't called when she said she would, he might not want her to call him at all. In one way she almost hoped he didn't. Then she wouldn't be responsible for calling the whole thing off. They could just not see each other again, and that would be that.

Perversely, the idea of never seeing Luke again gave her a twinge of pain. She had really liked him—and he had seemed to like her. In fact, Caprice wasn't sure that "like" was quite strong enough for the way she felt about Luke Banning. Naturally she didn't love him—she had reaffirmed that thought to herself for days. She only *liked* him . . . a lot.

"Are you going to dial that number, or do I have to do it for you?" Katie demanded.

"I thought you were against this scheme."

"At first I was, but now I've changed my mind. It just never occurred to me that you could pull it off. But you *did*. You not only got into the party and met him face to face, but he even kissed you! Now I have every confidence you can get him to marry you."

"Maybe it's wrong for me to do it. After all, this is his life, too. Maybe I don't have the right to stir it up."

"No right? I can't believe I'm hearing this! I worked at an engagement party until one o'clock this morning, and the hostess didn't even give us a bonus for overtime. She seemed offended that we took so long cleaning up afterward and even made a snippy comment about me being clumsy for accidentally spilling about a teaspoon of champagne on the rug. I was tired to the bone from being on my feet all day, and that's why I misjudged the glass. And champagne doesn't stain. If it had been burgundy she would probably have had me beheaded! No, Cappy, that bunch is fair game for anything we can put over on them."

Caprice frowned. "That sounds like Jed's attitude, not yours."

"I'm beginning to think he's right about some things. Why should the rich get richer, while we struggle to make ends meet?" Katie slouched in the faded armchair. "When I finally got home last night,

I went in to check on Heather and she was running a fever again. I was up with her off and on all night.''

"She seems all right today. Why didn't you wake me up?''

"You needed your sleep. A socialite doesn't go around with dark circles under her eyes. Now call Banning.''

Reluctantly Caprice dialed the number. Heather's needs took priority over Caprice's conscience.

When Luke answered on the second ring, Caprice almost hung up. She had expected a maid or butler to pick up the phone, and was caught off guard. "Luke?''

"Yes, who is this?'' His deep voice missed a beat. "Caprice?'' She could hear the surprise in his inflection.

"Yes. I'm sorry I didn't call you after the party, but I became unexpectedly tied up.''

Katie nudged Caprice and poked her nose toward the ceiling to indicate Caprice should sound more sophisticated. Caprice frowned at the suggestion.

"I'm glad you called. I didn't get your number the other night, and since you aren't listed, I didn't know how to find you.''

"I know. Or rather, I realized that after I had left,'' she amended. "Actually I'm rather difficult to catch at home, so I rarely give out my number. It's easier for me to call from here and there.''

"You're quite an enigma. I don't know anyone who can't be reached by phone.''

"I travel a great deal.'' Caprice saw Katie grin and nod vigorously. Caprice turned her back on his sister, but Katie shifted from the chair to the rocker so she wouldn't miss a single nuance.

"Are you in town now?"

"Why, yes. I am."

"Would you like to come over here for dinner?"

"Dinner? No, no, that would be too much trouble," she said before she thought. Katie already had supper cooking, and Caprice forgot for a minute that Luke had only to order his cook to prepare more.

"I wouldn't want to put you to any inconvenience," Luke said, completely misunderstanding what she had meant.

Katie punched Caprice's arm and glared at her sister as she shook her head.

"I didn't mean it like that. As a matter of fact, I would love to have dinner with you tonight."

"Good. I'll pick you up at eight, if that's all right with you."

"No, I'll come to your house. What's the address?"

"Number twelve Haven Brook. Are you sure you want to drive over? I don't mind coming after you."

"I'm going to be near there, and it's better if I just come over."

"I'll see you at eight then."

She said goodbye and hung up, her knuckles whitening as she continued to grasp the receiver. "I did it!"

"For a minute there I thought you were going to blow the whole thing. It sounded like you were turning down a date instead of doing the opposite."

Caprice didn't answer immediately. After a moment she said, "What happens when he insists on calling me here, or worse still, on driving me home?"

"Stall him. Spend the night if he won't let you call a cab."

"That's rather extreme, don't you think?"

"Good! Good! You said that with the perfect accent. As for him calling here, that's no problem. He can't see over the telephone line. He'll think I'm your servant."

"I'm going to call this whole thing off."

"You can't!"

"Why can't I?"

"Because I told Mr. Haynes that you're giving notice, and he got so upset he said for me to tell you that you're fired."

"What! Katie, why would you do a thing like that?"

"You can't keep serving at parties now. You'll be recognized. Even with brown hair, someone would notice you. Besides, you have to find a way to attend them as a guest. You have to insinuate yourself into that crowd before they know what's going on."

"So now I'm out of work again." Caprice stared at her sister.

"You don't need a job. We're going for the big bucks."

"I don't like the way that sounds. And just how do you plan to make ends meet on one salary until I marry this man? *If* it ever happens?"

"I'll think of something. We can sell your old Pontiac, for starters. You can't be seen driving one like that anyway, and it will bring more than the station wagon. As for Heather's doctor bills, I can put them off for a while. Once you're Mrs. Banning you can send me enough to get out of the hole."

Worry puckered Caprice's brow. She didn't like what Katie was saying. She sounded as heartless as she had so often described the wealthy. This was a side of her sister Caprice hadn't seen before.

Caprice dressed with care as Katie and Heather ate their supper. She purposely stayed out of the kitchen so the smell of home cooking wouldn't cling to her clothes. She dressed in a jade-green moiré suit with a slightly gathered skirt and short jacket over a simple white top. The fabric was a good replica of an expensive cloth and even an expert would have been hard-pressed to tell the difference. She left her hair down and brushed it into a flaming mane that rippled with glowing health. She borrowed Katie's gold ear studs and slipped her feet into her white sandals. By the time Katie and Heather came into the living room, Caprice had already called a taxi.

"You may as well put an ad in the paper about my car," Caprice agreed. "The starter's making a funny sound occasionally, and we can't afford to get it fixed. We should sell it before it gets any worse." She smoothed her niece's blond hair. "How do you feel, honey?"

"Okay, I guess. Mom's wearing the skin off my forehead feeling for a temperature."

"We care a lot about you."

"I know," Heather said with a child's confidence. "You look nice."

"Thanks. Katie, I borrowed your earrings. I couldn't show up without jewelry again."

"That's okay. I hear your taxi. Have a good time." Katie opened the door for her.

Caprice stepped out into Houston's sultry dusk. The days were still long and the air was too humid to cool off, even after dark. She got into the cab and said, "Number twelve Haven Brook, please."

The cabby turned to look at her as if he couldn't believe his ears. "Haven Brook? The one in River Oaks?"

"I don't think there is another one." She crossed her legs and gazed out the window in dismissal. Since she now had no job and would soon have no car, the scheme *had* to work. For a moment she traitorously wondered if Katie had consciously backed her into a corner so that she would have no choice but to go through with it. Caprice shook her head. She didn't want to believe that.

The cab driver negotiated the complicated freeway system and turned onto the Kirby exit and from there into a series of turns that ended on Haven Brook. He turned to look at her and asked, "Is this it, lady?"

She leaned forward and smiled. Unlike most of the houses, which leaned heavily toward French provincial, colonial, or Tudor, this one was Spanish. It was a long and rambling hacienda with a second story at the back. The traditional white stucco walls and red tiled roof, as well as the curving red brick drive, were shaded by huge live oaks. No one could ever mistake it for an inexpensive home, but it had none of the ostentatious trappings that Caprice had expected. The house was homey and inviting despite its size. "This is it," she told the driver.

She paid him and got out of the cab. For some reason she felt curiously at ease here, even though she had been so nervous about coming. The house, like its owner, was different.

She was somewhat surprised when Luke answered the door, having assumed everyone in River Oaks had live-in maids and butlers. He stepped aside as he said, "Welcome. I didn't expect you to come by cab."

"I sold my car before moving, and haven't bothered buying another one. I prefer not to drive, anyway." She stepped inside and smiled her appreciation of the view. "How lovely!"

The room was done in shades of sand, desert blues and silvers. Waist-high adobe walls led from the entry into a sunken living room. The floor was natural-hued quarry tile with a thick Navaho rug in front of the stone fireplace. Oversized, overstuffed muted blue and rose chairs and a cherry wood coffee table invited all visitors to relax and sit back.

"Christine says it's too 'John Wayne' for her tastes, but it's comfortable." He motioned for her to precede him and, as she did so, she tried not to stare at her surroundings, but rather appear as though she were accustomed to such grandeur.

"I thought we would eat on the patio," he said as he opened a door leading toward the back of the house.

The long room, glassed-in on three sides, provided an air-conditioned view of an enormous swimming pool. Banana trees flanking the pool rustled in the warm breeze. On each side were flower beds filled with purple and white vincas.

"*The Great Gatsby* goes western," she mused aloud.

"I know it's ostentatious, but it was like that when I bought it." He was watching her, rather than the softly illuminated outdoor scene. "Where have you been all week?"

Caprice looked up and found his quicksilver eyes studying her. "Oh, here and there. First one place, then another."

He nodded. "I have weeks like that, too."

A round slate-topped table had been set for two, with candles on each side of a low centerpiece. Caprice knew instinctively the gleaming flatware was sterling and not silver plate—far removed from Katie's dime-store stainless.

Luke held her chair for her, and as soon as he seated himself opposite her, a maid appeared with thick steaks, baked potatoes, and spinach salad.

"It's a good thing you're punctual," he said. "Juanita is leaving early tonight, and she was put out that I didn't tell her sooner that I was having company. I hope you like steak and potatoes."

"I do."

The maid reappeared with home-baked bread on a wooden board and a bowl of whipped butter. She glanced impersonally at Caprice but didn't make eye contact. Caprice was reminded of her own days as a caterer's waitress, but she remembered to remain aloof and not make eye contact either.

"Thanks, Juanita," Luke said with a smile. "Juanita bakes the best bread in town. Try some."

Caprice saw the woman smile and realized her lowered eyes were a mark of shyness rather than servility. She took a bite and said, "This *is* good."

Juanita nodded her thanks and left silently. "She doesn't speak much English," Luke explained once she was gone, "but she's learning fast. I'm afraid before long she'll be able to understand the offers Christine makes behind my back to lure her away."

"Christine would do that?"

"Sure. I stole her gardener the same way." With his usual rapid change of subject, he said, "Your eyes are as green as I remembered. I had thought perhaps my memory must have been exaggerated."

She looked up quickly. He wasn't eating, but was intently watching her. All at once she wasn't very hungry, either. Not with him gazing at her like that.

"Caprice, where have you really been? I've looked for you everywhere I've gone. None of my friends know you. I was beginning to think I had dreamed you."

"I was with my sister," she answered. When he looked at her with those eyes that seemed to see into her soul, she couldn't lie.

"Where does she live?"

"North of here." Being evasive wasn't easy with him.

"The Woodlands," he surmised. "It's nice up there."

"Yes, it is."

"I'm still amazed—I never knew that June has nieces. But then, she seldom talks much about herself since she's so interested in the Pin Oak Horse Show and her other clubs."

"That's Aunt June, all right."

They ate slowly. Caprice found it impossible not to look at Luke, and he seemed to be equally drawn to her. When they were finished, Juanita cleared away the dishes and brought each of them a generous serving of hot apple pie. Caprice couldn't keep a smile from her face; Katie probably thought they were dining on roasted pheasant and chocolate mousse.

"Why are you smiling?" he asked.

"Because you're so much nicer than I thought you'd be. And because this isn't mousse."

"You don't like mousse?"

"I have nothing against it, personally." She managed not to chuckle, though her eyes sparkled. She had never tasted mousse.

After they finished their dessert, they stood and walked over to a couch that matched the puffy chairs in the adjoining room. Caprice could hear the faint sounds of Juanita removing the last of the dishes.

"Do you always leave parties as abruptly as you did the other night?" he asked as he sat beside her.

"Not always."

"I found myself thinking of Cinderella, but there was no glass slipper and no sign of a pumpkin the next morning."

"I guess I got away in time," she said lightly.

"And vanished neatly into the fog from whence you came."

"That sounds more like a vampire than Cinderella," she said with a laugh.

"All the same, you're very hard to track down. Will you give me your sister's number?"

Caprice hesitated. The prefix wouldn't be correct for The Woodlands since the phone was a Heights number. On the other hand, how else could he call her? She wrote out the number on the back of one of his cards, and he slipped it under the nearby phone.

"Next time you're over, bring a swimsuit," he said. "We can go for a moonlight swim."

"Next time?"

"Or we can go for one tonight," he said as he rejoined her and slid his arm across the back of the couch.

Caprice swallowed nervously and pressed her clammy palms into the soft material of her skirt. He was bending so close she could feel his warm breath on her lips.

He reached up to touch her cheek and ran his fingers through her hair. "Juanita will be gone in a few minutes and no one can see over my wall."

"I've never...that is, I don't..."

"I know. You're not that kind of a woman," he said softly, his voice as much of a caress as his hand. "What kind are you?"

"I don't know how to answer," she finally managed to say. "I'm just myself."

He laughed quietly. "That's like saying the Hope Diamond is a piece of compressed coal. You look as seductive as hell, but I get the feeling I'll never see you again if I make a wrong move. My only trouble is figuring out which moves are the wrong ones."

Caprice felt herself drawn to him; his lips were compelling and too close to her own. She jumped up and walked hurriedly to the picture window. "That certainly is a nice pool," she said inanely as she tried to collect her wits. "Do you like to swim?"

There was a pause, and she closed her eyes to get better control of her body. When Juanita left, they would be alone in the house. Was this a man she could trust? He was really no more than a stranger to her. What if he forced himself on her? She jumped when his voice sounded close beside her.

"I love the water. I guess it comes from having a birthday in March under the sign of the fish." He pointed toward the far side of the pool. "I'm thinking of putting a cabana over there. Maybe with a couple of guest rooms. How do you think that would look?"

"Very handy," she said as she tried to calm her racing pulse.

"Handy. Yes, I guess that's true." He looked at her as if he simply couldn't figure her out at all. "Do I frighten you?"

"You scare me to death," she said without thinking.

"Why?"

She looked at him in confusion. How could she answer questions like these? He stood perfectly relaxed, his hands in his slacks pockets, not seeming at all threatening on the surface, but she could sense the strength of his lean, well-muscled body. "Because you aren't like anyone I've ever known. You don't do or say what I expect.''

''What do you expect?''

''I don't know.''

''Then I can see how that would be confusing.''

Again the air between them seemed to crackle with excitement. Caprice ached to step into his embrace and knew he was waiting only for a hint of her acquiescence. Hastily, she looked away.

''It reminds me of *The Great Gatsby*, too,'' he said.

''What?'' she asked in confusion.

''The pool, of course.''

''Of course.''

''You know, you confuse me, too. I know a lot of people and you aren't in the least like anyone I've ever met.''

''No?'' Her voice was barely more than a whisper.

''There's a mystery about you. Something I can't quite put my finger on. Even though I know we never talked until that night on the *Idlewild*, I have the strangest feeling that we've known each other for a long time.''

''How odd. When I first saw you, I thought the same thing.''

''But that's impossible, of course.''

''Yes.''

Despite his words, he looked unconvinced. An arc of automobile headlights on the far hedges told Caprice that Juanita was leaving for the night. She suddenly felt the emptiness of the house drawing them together. ''Who is your decorator?'' she asked brightly to break the bond between them.

"I don't have one. I just buy what I like. Are you afraid because we're here alone?"

"No!" she answered too quickly.

"I thought so," he said, as if her answer had been in the affirmative. "Would you be more comfortable if we went somewhere else?"

"Would you prefer that?"

"No."

Caprice found she wouldn't prefer it either. "I really don't like crowds."

"Neither do I, but I also don't like scaring my friends out of their wits." With great gentleness, he touched her arm. "You're trembling."

"That's not entirely from fear," she admitted softly. "In fact, there's not much fear there at all."

His hand rested on her shoulder as he let his thumb stroke the pulse point in her slender neck. "Then why are you trembling?"

Caprice tore her gaze from his. "I don't know how to answer your questions or what to say to you."

"I find you equally confusing. Perhaps if we talk about something trivial. Where did you go to college?"

"Wellesley...in Massachusetts," she said as she and Katie had planned.

"Is there another one?" he asked with a smile. "I went to college here at Rice University. Where were you born?"

"Here." She found her voice going soft again, because her answer was true, in more than one sense. She felt as if she had been born the day she met him.

"So was I. That makes us a very rare breed—native Houstonians. Most people who live here are transplants."

He looked at her as if he was trying to find the missing pieces to a puzzle. "Are you going to live with your sister, or will you be finding a place of your own?"

"I haven't decided yet."

"Caprice, when can I see you again?"

"What?" she whispered.

"I have a feeling you're about to bolt, just like the other night. I don't want you to get away without saying you'll see me again."

"I'm free tomorrow."

"Would you like to go to a museum? How about the zoo?"

"The zoo?" she asked with a surprised laugh. "I haven't been there in years."

"Then it's time you went." He stepped nearer and his eyes darkened. "Caprice, you make me want to say things that I'm afraid you won't be willing to hear."

"I . . . I have to go. No, really I do. I promised my sister I wouldn't be late. This is the first time in years that I've been in town long enough to really visit," she babbled as she went to the phone and shakily dialed the taxi company. "You know how demanding sisters can be."

"At least let me drive you," he protested.

"No, no. I love to ride in cabs. It's a thing with me. In fact, I'll meet you at the zoo. Say at two?" She gave his address to the switchboard operator.

"Why are you suddenly so nervous?"

She hung up and turned to face him. "Because I just figured out who I'm really afraid of, and it isn't you. If I don't leave, I'm liable to say or do something that I shouldn't."

"No, you aren't. Not that you shouldn't, anyway." He stepped nearer, but didn't touch her. He didn't have to. His proximity was enough to sear her nerve endings. "Not when we both feel the same way."

"Luke," she said softly, just to hear his name, feel it on her lips.

"I'd ask you to stay the night," he said, "but you would run away."

"My sister," she whispered.

A horn honked out front, and he frowned. "What was that cabbie doing? Hiding around the corner?"

She grabbed her purse and hurried to the door. He opened it, but caught her waist as she tried to pass him. "You *will* show up at the zoo, won't you?"

"Yes. Yes, I'll be there." She didn't dare let him kiss her, so she ran for the safety of the cab.

All the way to her house her thoughts skittered in confusion. Only one thing was perfectly clear: she had fallen in love with Luke Banning, and that hadn't been part of the plan.

Chapter Six

Caprice put on her jeans and a cool cotton pullover in a broad stripe design, and took a chance on having Katie drive her to the zoo to save cab fare. Katie let her out on the far side of Hermann Park, well away from the zoo's gate, and Caprice walked over the grassy parkland to merge with the crowd.

Luke was already waiting for her, and when she saw him, her steps faltered. He, too, was wearing jeans, and was even more handsome in casual clothes than she had expected him to be. The jeans fit tightly about his narrow hips, and his red shirt went perfectly with his dark hair and gray eyes.

"I was beginning to think you weren't coming," he said when only a few feet of pavement separated them.

"I'm not late."

"No, but I was afraid you wouldn't show up."

The crowd eddied about them like a current. Caprice and Luke stood still, gazing at each other as if a conversation that needed no words were taking place. She heard the babble of voices in the several languages common in Houston, but she was aware of only him. "I wouldn't have stayed away at all," she said at last.

He held out his hand to her and waited until she took it before escorting her through the gate. The sun was unmercifully hot, and soon Caprice could feel the heat of the pavement through the soles of her tennis shoes. As usual, off to the south a bank of clouds hovered on the horizon, but it promised only rain and no relief from the heat.

To escape the roasting air, they went into the dimly lit aviary. From inside the air-conditioned sanctuary, they observed brilliant birds in cages that replicated as closely as possible the birds' natural habitat. A group of Vietnamese passed by, talking loudly in their native tongue.

"Why do people assume they can't be seen or heard if they speak another language?" Luke wondered aloud as three of the children shoved past them.

"I don't know, but I've noticed the same thing. I wonder if we seem that way when we go abroad? I hope not."

"Unfortunately, we probably do. Which country is your favorite?"

"America," she replied with a smile.

"I meant which foreign one do you prefer to visit?"

Caprice, who had never been out of the country, and seldom out of the state, said, "I have no favorite, really."

"I think mine is England. I like the castles and all that history. Besides, the language situation is easier there than in, say, Germany or France."

"Do you speak German and French?"

"French better than German, and only enough to get around town and read a menu. Do you?"

"No, I had high school Spanish, but I've forgotten most of it."

"People in most places speak English these days." He pointed to a brilliantly colored parrot. "I saw a whole flock of those once in Africa. I'll never forget it."

"You've been to Africa?" she asked in amazement. To her, Africa was a far-off place on the map and the setting for Tarzan movies.

"It was several years ago. I went on a photographic safari. Have you ever been on one?"

Caprice shook her head.

"You should go. It's a lot of fun. You get to see all the wild game, but no one expects you to kill it. That's what I liked best about it. I think hunting for sport is wrong."

"So do I."

"We have a lot in common, don't we? I knew right away we would."

"Did you?" she asked with a smile. "I'm more surprised at it all the time."

They went out into the open aviary where the birds flew in relative freedom. A suspension bridge spanned a jungle setting and an artificial waterfall roared at one end of the enclosure.

"May I see you again tomorrow?" he asked as they crossed the bridge.

Caprice hesitated only an instant. "I have to fly up to Chicago tomorrow morning. It's business, and I can't postpone it." She smiled back at him. "I'll be home the next day. I'd like to see you when I'm back." She had concocted the Chicago trip because she was going to take Heather back to the doctor the next afternoon. Besides, she didn't want Luke to find her too easy to date.

"Would you like to see a play? I have season tickets, and *Fiddler on the Roof* is opening the day after tomorrow."

"That sounds like fun." Mentally she ran through an inventory of her sparse wardrobe. What could she wear to the theater?

As they left the cool interior of the aviary, the heat seemed even more oppressive. Luke bought them tall cups of lemonade, and they strolled by the monkey house to the row of big cats with hardly a lull in their conversation.

"It's such a shame to cage them," Luke said. "Zoos should be run like the wilderness reserve where the animals run free and the people are confined to cars."

"I guess after seeing them in the wild, this is pretty tame."

"But a lot more comfortable. African insects have to be seen to be believed."

He took her hand as they circled back by the rhinoceros and elephant pens. "You're easy to be with," he said as he matched his steps to hers.

"So are you." Although they were merely holding hands, his fingers surrounding hers triggered her desire for more. Even his slightest touch was enough to send her senses reeling. What would it be like to make love with him?

"What are you thinking?" he asked with characteristic unexpectedness.

"What?"

"You looked as if you had something on your mind."

"I...I was just wondering if the Norwoods have finished their croquet lawn."

Luke laughed. " 'Winston's Folly' would be a good name for it. No, he's still making changes and revisions. He's thought of a new way to sterilize dirt. And now that he knows there are different kinds of sand, he wants to know the qualities of each one."

"It must be costing him a small fortune."

"Probably." He was surprised when she withdrew her hand. "Is something wrong?"

"No," she said stiffly. "I was just looking at the buffalo." She knew she was wrong to blame Luke for his brother-in-law's spendthrift ways, but she couldn't help it. The money for that croquet lawn would probably more than pay for Heather's operation.

"You weren't looking at the buffalo. What's wrong?"

"I just think it's odd for them to turn their lawn into a croquet court. It seems extravagant."

"It is, but that's Winston. Of course it isn't their entire lawn, just a corner of it."

"The money would be better spent on, say, a charity case. Like an operation for a poor child, for instance." She knew she was on dangerous ground, and she didn't dare look at him.

"You're probably right. Look over there—it's the buffalo calf. I remember reading about it in the paper last week. It's big for a baby, isn't it?"

Caprice didn't dare reopen the subject. "His legs are almost as long as his mama's."

"You don't care much for Christine and Winston, do you?" he asked in a casual tone as he watched the gangling calf trying to find its dinner.

"I don't know them."

"Yet you went to their wedding reception?"

"I went with Aunt June and Uncle Howard."

"There are things about Winston that I don't like either, and Christine can also be a pain at times. I often think that if I weren't wealthy, I'd be the black sheep of the family."

"You? Why do you think that?"

"Because I think croquet lawns are ridiculous, and I don't like to have parties simply because of social debt, and because I secretly dislike both the ballet *and* classical music."

"Are you serious?" she asked with a laugh.

"I'm afraid so. You may as well know the worst about me up front. I can't tell *Swan Lake* from *The Sleeping Beauty*. After half an hour of Beethoven I start to grit my teeth."

"I don't like those things either. I wouldn't have a party where I had to invite people who weren't my friends."

"No? How do you get around it?"

Her smile stiffened. "I move around a lot. A rolling stone gathers neither moss nor commitments."

"Some commitments are good."

She began walking slowly. By the tone of his voice and the way his fingers tightened almost imperceptibly about hers, she knew he meant something more personal than commitments in general. She almost hoped he didn't, however. Now that she knew him, she couldn't see him merely as a means of getting the money she needed. Luke was sensitive and caring, and she didn't want to use him. She had really hoped he would be shallow or have some giant personality flaw so she could continue to lump him in with the infamously careless upper class.

"You said you graduated from Wellesley. What year?"

"Why?"

"I was wondering if you knew Luana Beaufort while you were in school. She graduated from there, too."

"No, I don't know any Beauforts."

Luke looked at her quizzically. Luana belonged to every club in River Oaks and was close friends with June Walters. How could Caprice not know her?

They left the zoo and wandered past the miniature railroad to the Museum of Natural Science. "Seen any dinosaurs lately?" he asked.

"If it's cool in there, I'll look at anything," she said with a laugh. "Actually I have a soft spot in my heart for dinosaurs. At one time I wanted to be an archaeologist."

"Why didn't you?"

"I entered the ninth grade and discovered boys instead." She led him to where the bones of a brontosaurus soared three floors high. "Can't you just imagine walking through the woods and seeing one of these? That must have been an awe-inspiring sight."

"Not as awe-inspiring as the tyrannosaurus rex." Luke nodded toward the skeleton of the huge carnivore. "You would nearly fit into his mouth, feet and all."

"What a pity no one has invented a time machine so we can see what they really looked like. Or pop in on Patrick Henry's speech or see Elizabeth I's coronation...buy a Van Gogh or two before his prices went up."

"Ah, so your romanticism has a practical twist," he teased.

"Naturally. You can't live entirely on romance."

"Can't you?"

Caprice turned away. At one time she had told Katie that she was pessimistic enough to be practical. If she listened to Luke for very long, she would be neither. "Let's go downstairs and see the planetary exhibit."

"You know this museum pretty well for someone who hasn't lived here long."

"I grew up here. I just haven't lived here lately," she said quickly.

"The exhibit is fairly new."

"I guess I read about it or heard someone mention it." She silently chastised herself. If she made too many slips, he would become suspicious.

"You may have dreamed of digging up bones," he confided as they neared the exhibit, "but I once planned to go in the opposite direction. I wanted to be an astronaut and explore the stars."

"Why didn't you?"

"I grew too tall. For a while the requirement was that astronauts be under six foot and I passed that my junior year in high school. The restrictions are less stringent now, but they still don't want someone six foot four."

She smiled. "So millions won't buy everything?"

"They won't buy a lot of things. Like love." He looked at her in an odd way. "That's a strange thing for you to say—about millions not buying everything."

Mentally she scolded herself for making another slip. Being constantly on her guard wasn't easy. "On the other hand, some say it buys love."

"They're wrong. Nothing buys love."

"I guess you have to earn that."

"No, you have to be able to give it."

She looked at him quickly, but he seemed to be studying a mock-up of the planetary system.

"We always seem to revert back to the subject of love," she said as she looked at close-up photos of Jupiter's moons. "Why is that?" Her eyes met his over the top of the colored plates.

Luke only smiled. He wasn't sure she wouldn't run away if he answered that. He knew what he felt for her was sure and true, yet he was logical enough to know it was too soon to tell her. If he had learned one thing from Paulette, it was to bide his time and be certain before he spoke his mind. Not that Caprice was anything at all like his ex-wife. But sometimes his wealth was more like a Siamese twin than a belonging—he couldn't get rid of it long enough to see how people would view him without it. Fortunately Caprice was wealthy in her own right, and money was not the attraction.

He relaxed and let himself enjoy the pleasure of being near her. He wanted to make every minute count.

The doctor wasn't at all encouraging about Heather's prognosis. Caprice tried to convince him, in every logical way she knew, to let them pay off the surgery in installments. But Dr. Granger was adamant that such a plan was out of the question. The policy was set by the hospital administrators and he had to abide by it.

"If I make an exception for you, then everybody will expect the same leniency," he said.

"What's wrong with that?" Caprice countered, as Katie looked on in misery.

"Miss Dolan, I sympathize with your plight, but I have to earn a living, and the hospital has to stay in business."

"At two hundred thousand per operation, I'd say you both do very well."

Dr. Granger smiled frostily. "My fees aren't negotiable. In an operation of this sort, there are enormous expenses that you couldn't possibly be aware of."

"Such as? I'm sure the liver donor isn't charging you for the use of it."

"A remark in rather poor taste, all things considered. Actually there is the expense of removing the liver, transporting it, and placing it in the patient. There are hospital costs for the operating room, the intensive care unit, the hospital room, medication, anesthesia, et cetera. You can see how it adds up."

"I can understand that the operation is expensive, but I can't see why half of it must be paid up front."

Katie tugged at her sister's sleeve. "Caprice, please. Let's go. Heather will be getting restless in the waiting room."

"Frankly, Miss Dolan, it's because too many people, especially those in financial straits, refuse to pay anything at all." His pale eyes met Caprice's; he seemed to be enjoying his advantage.

"I wonder if you would be as rude to a Banning or a Norwood," Caprice said angrily.

"That's neither here nor there," he replied in a bored tone as he began shuffling papers to signal their dismissal. "I see a patient, not a bank account."

"Do you, doctor? When I look at Heather, I see a girl who may not be alive a year from now just because we don't have an extra two hundred thousand dollars in the bank!"

"Caprice, come on!" Katie grabbed her sister's wrist and stood up as she urged her toward the door.

Caprice let herself be led out before she lost her temper entirely. Once they were in the hall, she began, "What a pompous..."

"Hush. His nurse might hear you. We need him to perform this operation. I'm already behind on the payments for the tests. What if he refused to see Heather again?"

"You're right," Caprice said reluctantly. "I just hate to be put down."

"Life is like that," Katie said with a shrug. "People who have money are a breed apart from people who don't."

Only a week before, Caprice would have agreed. Now she knew Luke Banning, and she knew Katie was wrong. "People are people. Luke certainly isn't like that," she said in his defense.

"You don't know him very well. I've been observing these people for years, and believe me, they're all snobs."

"Not Luke," Caprice repeated stubbornly. "He's really nice."

"Cappy, don't get carried away with this. I know you need to like him a little in order to go through with the plan, but don't let him snow you. If he knew who you really are, he wouldn't give you a second glance."

Caprice's frown deepened, but she couldn't deny her sister's assertion. Certainly she dared not risk proving Katie wrong. As they met Heather in the waiting room, the thought crossed Caprice's mind that Katie might be jealous. Right away she dismissed the notion from her mind. Katie was her sister, and certainly loved Caprice unselfishly enough not to be jealous of her and Luke. All the same, Katie was unusually silent as they drove home.

Caprice wore the green moiré skirt and white blouse to the play and hoped Luke wouldn't recognize it without the matching jacket. She knew most men paid very little attention to women's clothes, and she figured Luke probably would be no exception.

"I'm glad you wore that skirt again," he said as they were leaving the theater. "It's the same color as your eyes."

"Thank you," she said simply and let it go at that. There was no plausible explanation as to why she would wear the same dress on two occasions in a row.

"I still wish you had let me pick you up. The Woodlands isn't all *that* far out of town."

"Of course it is. Besides, I like cabs, remember?"

"You may be the only person in the world who does."

"I guess it's just one of my quirks."

"Would you like to stop by the Pegasus for a drink?"

"That sounds nice." Caprice had seen the restaurant, but had never been inside it.

Luke drove through the streets. Despite the late hour, the traffic was still heavy. "You know," he said with deceptive casualness, "if I didn't know better, I would wonder if you might not have a husband stashed away in The Woodlands."

"A what?" she asked in genuine surprise.

"Think about it—you won't let me take you home or pick you up. I've never met your sister or even heard her name. Doesn't that sound a little suspicious?''

"Her name is Katherine, and I have never been married. If you don't believe me, call the number I gave you and ask her." She gave him Katie's real name because it sounded more elegant. "It never occurred to me that you might think I was married!"

"It was only a passing thought, not an overriding suspicion. If you were married, you'd be taking too big a chance by giving me your phone number. Obviously you don't have anything to hide or you wouldn't be seen with me in public." He smiled at her in the glow of the passing street lights.

"Right."

They pulled into the Pegasus parking lot, and the car rolled to a stop beside a large red oleander. Caprice waited for him to come around and open her door, then hand in hand they went into the building. The decor was predominantly blue with a galaxy of white stars overhead. Each wall featured a beautifully painted Pegasus either in flight or prancing through a cloudscape.

They sat in the bar and ordered drinks before Luke said, "I hope you aren't upset with me for asking if you're married."

"I'm not. I can see why you would wonder."

"My ex-wife taught me a lot along those lines. I think Paulette had affairs with half the men in town. Even now I don't know the whole sordid list."

"I'm not like that."

"I know you aren't, but she hurt me, and I had to be sure about you."

Caprice leaned forward and put her hand over his. "You're so vulnerable in some ways. I worry about you getting hurt."

"I can take care of myself."

"I know, but that doesn't keep you from being vulnerable."

"Is it that obvious?"

"Probably not to everyone. When you look at me, I can see a gentleness in your eyes."

He smiled and matched her palm to his before enclosing it in his clasp. "I don't open up this way with everybody. Very few people, in fact."

"Why me, Luke?"

"I think it's because I'm falling in love with you."

Caprice stared at him, unable to respond as their drinks arrived. Luke looked at her and then calmly paid the waitress as if he had merely made a comment about the weather.

"What did you say?" she asked when the waitress left.

He paused for a minute as he gazed into her eyes. "I love you, Caprice."

She swallowed nervously. These were the words she needed to hear, but all she could think of was the gentleness in Luke's silver eyes.

"If you want to run away, there's a pay phone by the door where you could call a cab. I should warn you, though, that if you do, I'll follow you."

Slowly she shook her head. "I don't want to run." She saw the flash of relief in his eyes. This had all happened so much faster than she had expected. If she were going to back out, she had to do it now. "I love you, too," she heard herself saying. Her heart had spoken before her conscience could stop her. She had been prepared to say the words from the beginning, but now she discovered they were true. She really did love Luke, and Heather had nothing to do with it. "I love you," she repeated softly.

"I know everyone will say we're rushing into this too fast." His eyes caressed her face as if he would like nothing better than to sweep her away and make love with her for a lifetime. "You know we're going to hear that."

She nodded, her own eyes misty with heartfelt emotion. "Maybe we are, Luke. After all, we've only known each other a short time."

"That may be true by the calendar, but we were never really strangers."

"I know. Luke, don't rush into anything you may regret later. You don't know anything about me."

"Do you have skeletons in your closet? What could they possibly matter to us? A husband is the only thing that could keep us apart. I haven't met your sister, but I know your aunt and uncle, and we're both of age so we don't need family approval. Are your parents spies or wanted for crimes in more than three states?"

"No," she said with a wavery laugh. "They're both dead."

"Do you have some incurable disease that will snuff you out tomorrow?"

"No."

"Are *you* a spy or wanted in more than three states?"

"No, I don't even know anyone who is."

Luke gestured as if he had proven his point. "Then there isn't anything we can't work out. Caprice, marry me. We can spend the next fifty years smoothing out the problems. I'll even take you for rides in cabs."

"Marry you?" she whispered.

"Is there any reason to wait?"

Caprice tried to think logically. This was what she had set out to accomplish, but now her love for him made her reluctant to say yes. The paradox was painfully confusing. "I don't know what to say."

"If you really love me, you know what to say. If you don't, then I'll keep courting you until you do love me. But I love you too much to let you go."

"Yes, Luke. Yes, I'll marry you." Her voice trembled as she added, "No matter what ever comes between us, please believe me. I truly do love you."

Luke bent over and kissed her with total disregard for the people around them.

Chapter Seven

Ralph, congratulate me. She said yes!" Luke grinned broadly at his friend and financial manager.

"Did she? To what question?" Ralph looked up from the papers he was sorting and peered myopically at Luke, who was sitting in one of the leather chairs across from his desk.

"We're going to be married. We set the date for August nineteenth."

"That's next week!" Ralph stared at Luke, his mouth dropping open.

"There's no need to wait. All we need is time to get the license. Call Reverend Barstow and arrange for the service. It's to be private. Just our immediately families. Then contact Captain Tolliver and tell him to get the *Idlewild* ready to sail to the Mediterranean."

"Luke, you can't be serious!"

"I know it's hot at this time of the year, but I think it's the most romantic place to take a bride."

"Forget the weather report! You can't marry a perfect stranger!"

"She's probably not perfect, but she's damned close," Luke said lightly.

"Be serious. And get that sappy grin off your face! You're making a big mistake here."

"No, I'm not. You're only saying that because you haven't met her. She's perfect for me."

"How do you know? You've barely had time to get to know her. Can you tell me her middle name?"

"No, but I'll ask her. Is that your only objection?" Luke grinned even more broadly and picked up a heavy glass paperweight containing a replica of an oil well.

"As your manager, I have to counsel you not to do this!"

"As your boss, I'm overriding your advice." Luke turned the paperweight around as he studied the tiny details of the structure.

"Give me that before you break it." Ralph took back the paperweight and carefully rearranged the papers on his already tidy desk so they lined up parallel to its leather inset.

"When you begin to look irritated instead of just sounding that way, I know you're upset. What's bothering you?"

"What's bothering me? What do you think?" Ralph scowled at Luke through his thick glasses.

"Didn't you learn anything from your first marriage?"

"I sure did. Caprice is nothing at all like Paulette."

"I'm not talking personalities here. Let me put this to you gently and see if you can grasp it. You're the richest bachelor in town, or at least one of the top two."

"Yes, that's probably true."

"Any woman who marries you will be financially set for life."

"Most men do support their wives. You're right again."

"All this woman has to do is marry you, get a divorce, and be a millionairess!"

"Not entirely. In the first place, Caprice isn't marrying me as a career move. In the second, the courts would only award her a portion of whatever accrued after the marriage."

"And you're about to sign a deal with Ehud ben Yaron that will net you another two million!"

"Right again. Calm down, Ralph. Caprice and I are in love. She isn't after my money."

"You can't possibly know that."

"You've never been in love. I trust her."

Ralph frowned at Luke and picked up a newly sharpened pencil and laid it beside the papers, aligning it precisely. "I want to do a background investigation on her."

"Absolutely not! Are you out of your mind? I'm marrying her, not hiring her."

"All the more reason for a thorough investigation. You can't fire a wife."

"No."

"If we had checked into Paulette's personal life, we would have discovered her...shall we say, proclivities?"

"Caprice isn't like that either."

"You mean you haven't..."

"That's none of your business. Just take my word for it. Caprice isn't a sex addict like Paulette." He had secretly been rather glad to see that Caprice was thus far avoiding the bed. Finding a woman with old-fashioned morals was a relief after Paulette's promiscuity.

"Maybe you should worry about having the opposite problem with this one," Ralph suggested dryly.

"Not a chance." Caprice's passionate kisses eliminated the possibility of hang-ups when it came to sex. She just had principles.

"Well, you're at least going to have her sign a prenuptial agreement, aren't you?"

"No, I'm not."

"Oh, yes, you are. As your financial manager, I *do* have a say in that. I propose an allowance of, say, three thousand a month."

"Don't be silly, Ralph. Christine spent that much at Neiman-Marcus last week."

"I'm not the Norwoods' manager. I'm yours."

"Then make it five thousand a month." When he saw the stubborn set to Ralph's expression, he added, "I won't agree to a penny less. Hell, Ralph, I can afford it."

"That's not the point."

"I won't be stingy with her. Five thousand."

"Okay, but she also has to agree not to ask for more than forty percent of the assets accrued since the marriage, in the case of a divorce."

"You can be a pain in the neck, did you know that?"

Ralph gave Luke an angelic smile. "I know. That's one reason you're the richest bachelor in town."

"All right," Luke said with resignation. "We'll do it your way. Draw up the agreement. But make it tactful."

"Luke, I'm just looking out for you. I'm not trying to be hard-nosed and pessimistic."

"Yes you are. That's why I hired you. Okay, we'll do things your way, but I can tell you now that after you meet her, you're going to feel pretty silly for not trusting her."

"Will I? That should be a new experience for me."

Luke stood up and went to the office door. "Be sure you make arrangements with the preacher and Captain Tolliver."

"I'm not likely to forget that. Will there be a reception afterward?"

"Just a small one for the wedding guests. There's no need to cater it. Juanita and the cook can handle that many. We'll have it here." He smiled again as he said, "Have Doneby's Jewelers bring out a tray of rings. Tell him to put in some emeralds as well as diamonds. Her eyes are green."

Ralph shook his head dismally, but he jotted down the instructions. "Anything else?"

"That's it for now. I'll call my parents and Christine. Caprice can tell me tonight how many she plans to invite. I'll let you know tomorrow."

"Okay, boss."

"Cheer up. This is a wedding, not a wake." Luke waved as he left the office.

For a moment Ralph sat there in thoughtful silence. He knew Luke was rushing into this. The man was spontaneous and trusting to a fault. Ralph knew Luke had long since forgotten it, and certainly Ralph would never remind him, but he had suggested that Luke investigate Paulette as well.

He tapped the pencil's eraser lightly on the desk. As Luke's friend as well as manager, Ralph had a responsibility to him. Without further qualms, he lifted the heavy Yellow Pages directory onto his desk and leafed through the pages. Luke had said he would do it Ralph's way, and Ralph decided to take that as a directive. He found the number he was looking for, and punched it into his phone with staccato accuracy.

"Hello, Morris? This is Ralph Slayton. Just fine, thanks. Listen, I have a matter I want you to check out for me. No, this is a personal one. Her name is Caprice Dolan, and she lives in The Woodlands. Dolan, that's right. Just tell me what you can about her background and what sort of person she is. Okay, Morris. I'll be talking to you."

Ralph hung up and looked for a moment at the telephone. His conscience bothered him a bit, but not so much that he was sorry for having called Morris Ainsley. If nothing suspicious turned up, Luke need never know the investigation had been run. If Ralph's intuition proved correct—and he sincerely hoped he was wrong—Luke needed to know.

He dialed the number of the yacht to schedule the honeymoon cruise as Luke had ordered.

"He proposed!" Katie said with a triumphant shriek. "When are you getting married?"

"The nineteenth. I was able to convince him to have a simple ceremony with just the immediate family."

"We can't possibly go!"

"I know. I'll have to tell him you're out of town on business or something."

"You should never have told him we exist at all."

"How could I lie about everything? This isn't as easy as you seem to think. I have to watch every word I say. Besides, I had to have someplace to say I'm living, some address, however vague. If I told him I had my own house, he would expect to be asked over."

"Won't he anyway?"

"I don't know, Katie." Caprice nervously paced the room. "I don't see how we can possibly make this work. I want to back out."

"You can't do that! Not when we're so close!"

"Don't you understand? He isn't a faceless person anymore. It was easy for me to decide to marry a millionaire for Heather's sake, but now I *know* him. I don't want to hurt him."

"You're not hurting him, for goodness' sake. You're helping Heather. Cappy, bills are mounting up fast. My salary isn't enough to feed us and keep the electricity on, much less to pay for Heather's medical expenses. I'm already getting nasty notes from Dr.

Granger's receptionist. What if they cancel her next appointment?''

''I know, I know!'' Caprice stopped pacing and pressed her fingertips against her throbbing temples. ''I'm getting a headache.''

''Take two aspirin and get dressed. You don't want to be late for your date. I'll make you a tuna sandwich to eat while you're waiting for the cab.''

''Okay.'' Caprice undressed and showered quickly. On one hand she wanted to call it all off, but on the other she couldn't bear the idea of not seeing Luke again. Her love for him was growing so alarmingly fast that he had become an obsession. All her daytime thoughts centered on him, and he was the subject of all her dreams at night.

She put on a pale blue dress with a white lace collar. If she married Luke—when she married him—how would she explain her lack of a wardrobe? She didn't know where or even if he had planned a honeymoon, but even if they never left Houston she would need more than three nice dresses and a few pairs of casual slacks. She didn't even have working clothes to fall back on, because she never worked in Swayse's showroom and had therefore dressed very casually at the shop.

Then there was the matter of her nightgowns and underwear. In both cases they were made of cotton. She might be able to bluff her way through the ceremony with her handful of dresses, but the first time she undressed, he was bound to wonder. At least, she thought wryly, her lack of silk and lace undergarments had kept her chaste. Certainly it wasn't for lack of desire. When Luke kissed her, she wanted him so badly she ached. She hoped her car would sell soon so she would have money for a trousseau.

Once more she took a cab to his house and begrudged every cent. This money was needed so much in so many other places that she felt guilty spending it despite the necessity.

Luke opened the door and ushered her into the living room. "I had Ralph make arrangements for the wedding," he said as they sat on the couch. "Is the Mediterranean all right with you?"

"All right for what?" She was still trying to figure why the cab driver had charged her a dollar more than the ride had cost before.

"For our honeymoon, of course. Would you rather fly somewhere? I never thought to ask if you get seasick. I just assumed you'd prefer to sail."

Caprice stared at him. "We're going to the Mediterranean?"

"I take the *Idlewild* across the ocean with no problem at all. A yacht that size is pretty steady sailing. Is seasickness a problem with you?"

"I don't know. I've never sailed before."

"What?" he asked with a laugh.

"Well, I mean I've *sailed*," she amended hastily, "but never across an entire ocean. Are you serious about us going to the Mediterranean?"

"Unless you'd rather go somewhere else. Do you like Lisbon? I thought we would see it, skip over to Palma, then cross over to Pisa and Naples and then to Athens. How does that sound?"

Caprice stared at him as if he were suggesting they fly to Jupiter with a side excursion to Mars. "Fine," she managed to say.

"Do you have any favorite spots you'd like to visit while we're there?"

"No, no. That all sounds wonderful. All the way to Athens, Greece?"

He laughed. "I hoped you'd be pleased. Don't worry about seasickness. There are medications for it. If you've never been sick on the Walters's yacht, you probably won't be on ours. The *Idlewild* is larger than the one Howard keeps."

"I've never had seasickness on the Walters's yacht," she said in a small voice. "Luke, are you sure you want to marry me? *Really* sure, I mean? You know so little about me."

"You can tell me the rest on the way to Athens." He leaned nearer and kissed the pulse that beat in her throat.

Caprice murmured as a hot wave flowed through her. He slipped his arm about her waist and drew her closer to him, his lips blazing a trail of aching desire up the column of her throat. "Luke," she whispered with longing in her voice, "I love you so much."

"Are you sure? Maybe you want to wait awhile and be more certain." His voice was velvety as he nuzzled her ear. "Are you sure you love me? I don't want to rush you."

"I know I love you with all my heart. I have no doubts about that. Do you?"

"None at all. If I had any doubt at all, I would be asking you to wait. When we get married, I want it to be forever."

"Forever?" she whispered. How could she keep her background a secret for the rest of her life?

"You know I've been through one divorce. I don't want to do that again. If you can't say this feels like a permanent commitment, I have to know."

"All I know is that I'll never stop loving you. How can I guarantee that the marriage will last?"

"If you love me, it will." He brushed his lips over her cheek, and she turned her mouth to meet his.

Caprice's senses reeled as he kissed her expertly. She loved him, and she knew this was a love that would last forever, but what if he found out she wasn't at all who he thought she was? In the beginning she hadn't planned to stay married to him any longer than it took to get the money for Heather's operation. But loving him as much as she did, how could she leave him? Especially now that she didn't want to hurt him and knew that he loved her. She had never been so confused in her life.

"There is one thing my manager insisted upon," Luke said. "I think it's ridiculous, but when you get to know Ralph you'll understand. He insists we sign a prenuptial agreement."

"A what?"

"All it says is that in the event of a divorce, we divide only the money and property accrued since the wedding, and that you have an allowance of five thousand a month."

"Five *thousand*?" Caprice gasped.

"Is it enough? I may be able to squeeze more out of him. After we've been married a while, I know he'll relax a little. In some ways he's much too conservative."

"Five thousand?" she repeated, incredulous. "Every month?"

"Is there a problem with it? What would make you happy?"

"No, no, there's no problem." She took the paper and read it quickly. "Where do I sign? Do we need a notary?"

"No, Ralph will have to be happy with a simple signature. Of course it's worded so that your income and possessions are also protected. I dislike the idea of prenuptial agreements. They make getting married seem like a business venture. Are you upset?"

"No, of course not. I can understand Ralph wanting to protect you." She took a pen from him and quickly signed her name. At five thousand a month, she would find it difficult to get the hundred thousand for the operation's down payment, but this put her closer than she had been before. Maybe with that kind of income, the doctor would reconsider monthly payments.

The sound of the doorbell made her jump. "Are you expecting company?"

"It's probably the man from Doneby's. We need to pick out your wedding ring."

"Here?" she exclaimed. "They're bringing the rings out here?" She was feeling more and more like Alice in Wonderland. These things didn't happen in real life. Already Luke was opening the door and admitting a small man with a large briefcase handcuffed to his wrist and a uniformed guard at his side.

"This is Mr. Smythe," Luke said.

She nodded hesitantly. "Nice to meet you."

The guard unlocked the handcuff from Mr. Smythe's wrist and backed away. At the small man's nod, his escort stepped out and closed the door behind him. Mr. Smythe sat on a chair across the coffee table from the couch and carefully set the case on the table as if it and all its contents were too precious for mortal eyes. "Mr. Doneby sent out a wide variety of rings. Naturally if you have a particular design in mind, we can make it up to order." He unlocked the case, opened it and laid it flat. Taking out a midnight-blue velvet tray, he lay the first ring on it and pursed his lips as Caprice caught her breath.

She was afraid to touch it. The diamond was so large it looked like an imitation rather than the real thing.

"Too big," Luke said. "Caprice has small hands. See? It would cover the whole joint."

"Yes," she agreed fervently. She would be afraid to wear a ring like that out of the house.

"Here's a nice one," Mr. Smythe said as he extracted a splashy arrangement of baguettes. "The wedding ring fits in the center of the engagement ring and the set makes an elegant dinner ring."

"Don't you have any plain gold bands?" Caprice asked.

Mr. Smythe looked at her as if she were speaking a language he didn't recognize.

"Do you like jewelry?" Luke asked. "It suddenly occurred to me that you never wear any."

Caprice didn't know what to say. "Yes, I like jewelry. But these are so..." She wanted to say expensive, but she felt that would be an awkward objection under the circumstances.

"...so flashy," Luke finished for her. "I agree. What else do you have? I asked for some emeralds to be sent out."

"We have this one." Mr. Smythe removed the set and brought out another one. A square-cut emerald solitaire was set into the engagement ring. The wedding band was a spray of diamond baguettes that fanned around half the large green stone when the two rings were together.

Luke smiled and nodded. "That's more like it. What do you think, honey?"

Caprice could only stare. She had never seen such a beautiful ring. Realizing he was waiting for her answer, she reverently took it from the tray and slipped it onto her finger. Even the fit was perfect. The emerald in its diamond skirt glowed against her skin. "It's so beautiful!"

"We'll take this one," Luke said decisively.

"No, Luke! I mean, it's so expensive!" She couldn't possibly let him spend so much money.

"Do you like it?" he asked.

"Of course I like it. That's not the question."

"Do you think you'll get tired of an emerald? Diamonds are more versatile, I guess."

She could tell this was the one he preferred as well. "Green is my favorite color. I wouldn't get tired of it."

"That settles it. Mr. Smythe, tell Doneby that I appreciate his accommodating me by sending you out."

"Yes, sir. Glad to oblige." Mr. Smythe started folding the case up and handed Luke a blue velvet box.

"Luke," she tried again to object. "I had expected something much plainer."

"That's the wonderful thing about money. You don't have to settle for plain. Besides," he grinned, "it fits."

She sat staring at the ring as he signed the necessary papers and showed the man to the door. In all her wildest fantasies, this scenario had never occurred to her.

When he walked back into the room, she said, "You didn't even ask how much it cost! Luke, call him to come back and let's be reasonable about this."

"Ralph will have taken care of that. Doneby's knew what price range I expect. I've dealt with them in the past." He laughed at the puckered lines on her forehead. Paulette, and probably Christine as well, would have gone for the ostentatious ring Smythe had presented first. Luke found it marvelously refreshing that Caprice wasn't interested in having the most expensive one just because it was offered.

He held her hand so that the lights sparkled in the stones. "It's beautiful. Like you are. I told him to send emeralds because they remind me of your eyes."

"Luke," she sighed softly. "You're much too good to me."

"I'm going to do everything in my power to make you happy."

"All I ask is that you let me love you."

"Don't you even ask for love in return?"

She shook her head. "I love you so much that there's enough love for both of us."

"That's the way I feel about you." He enclosed her hand in his and leaned nearer until only a breath separated them. "Stay with me tonight, Caprice."

"I . . . I can't." She suddenly recalled her cotton underwear, and hysterical laughter threatened to overcome her. People who wore emerald and diamond rings didn't wear cotton panties from a discount store! The laughter bubbled out, and she leaned her forehead against his.

"I never had that reaction before when I asked someone to spend the night."

She laughed harder. How had Caprice Dolan from the Heights gotten herself into this? Her laughter was contagious, and Luke chuckled as she collapsed against him.

"Tell me one thing," he said when she tried to get her breath. "Why are we laughing?"

That sent her into another helpless peal. "I'm just so happy!" she said between bursts.

He pulled her back against him and half lay on the couch with her curled by his side. "I've heard of women crying and saying that, but not laughing. When you think about it, I guess this makes more sense."

"No, it doesn't, but I love you."

"I wonder if I'll ever understand you."

"Probably not," she said as she tried to compose herself.

"If you're this happy over spending one night, wait until you hear this one. Move in with me. Now. There's no need to wait until the wedding."

The smile left her face. "I can't do that."

"Why not?"

"How...how could I explain it to my sister?" she asked lamely. She needed the week to sew up a believable trousseau, and she certainly couldn't do that here.

"If your sister is over sixteen, and I assume she is, she should be able to understand it. These days many people live together before they're married."

"Katherine is very...religious. She would be too upset, and her opinion is important to me."

Luke sighed. "I guess I can wait a week, but it's not easy."

Caprice slowly eased the rings from her finger and put the diamond wedding band in the velvet box. "Luke, have you made that offer to very many women who didn't laugh? About spending the night, I mean?"

"No," he replied as he took the emerald and slipped it back on her finger. "Casual affairs have never interested me. How about you? Have you had similar good laughs in the past?"

"I've never been with anyone."

"Never?"

"I know I'm old-fashioned, but I never wanted anyone enough to give myself to him."

"Lady, you're exactly the person I've been looking for all my life." He understood now why she hadn't gone to bed with him, and he admired her for it.

Caprice tilted her head and kissed him, first gently, then with more passion. She wished with all her might that she had thought of some way to buy nice underwear so she didn't have to sound so prudish.

"How many should I tell Ralph to arrange for at the reception?"

"None of my family can make it. There's only my sister and her daughter." Suddenly remembering, she hastily added, "That is, since Aunt June and Uncle Howard are in Turkey. And Katherine is leaving town tomorrow and won't be back before the wedding."

"She won't fly back for it? I can't meet her until we come home from our honeymoon?"

"Perhaps not even then," Caprice said, suddenly inspired. "She may be moving to Canada."

"What on earth for?"

"Business. You know how it is. Most of her enterprises are there, and it would be handier for her to be nearer to them."

"What sort of business is she in?"

"Kiss me, Luke. I really don't want to talk about her."

With a trusting smile, he was glad to comply.

Chapter Eight

Luke, I cannot believe you are actually going through with this," Ada Banning said, her gray head held stiffly erect.

"Marrying someone we've never even met!" Christine seconded.

"We know her aunt and uncle. Caprice came to your wedding reception."

"How could she when I don't even know her? Winston, do you know this Caprice Dolan?" When her husband shook his head, she said, "See!"

Albert Banning came to stand behind his wife and frowned at his son. "You mother and sister are right. It's not the thing for you to do. In our family, we don't marry strangers."

"Would you like to meet her? I'll call and have her come over." Luke was trying to be reasonable, but his patience was wearing thin.

"No," Ada said firmly. "Even if we met her, we wouldn't *know* her. I've never once heard June or Howard mention a niece."

"She says they aren't especially close."

"Why is that?" Christine said. "You aren't implying she's from a poor branch of the family! With your money, you have to be careful."

"I'm implying nothing of the kind. I thought you'd be happy that I'm finally settling down. Goodness knows you've all tried hard enough to match me up with every eligible woman in town."

"I've done no such thing," his mother snapped guiltily. "You needn't act like one of your father's side of the family." Albert's money had been made by his father, a fact that classified him as nouveau riche compared to Ada's family, which had been wealthy for generations, and Ada never let him forget that he had attended public schools.

Albert's frown deepened as if he didn't want to claim Luke either. "He may be named after my father, but he gets his hardheadedness from your people."

"Please," Christine said in exasperation. "Not now. It doesn't matter who Luke takes after. What matters is whether or not he marries this Dolan person."

"I don't need your permission," Luke reminded them with deceptive calmness. "Caprice and I are in love, and we are going to be married."

"You're rushing into something you'll regret," Ada said.

"I, for one, won't sanction the ceremony with my presence. Neither will Winston," Christine said with a jerk of her head. "You'll have to get married without us."

"Neither will we," Ada said. "We won't come."

For a moment there was heavy silence in the room. Then Luke went over to the phone and dialed Ralph's extension. "Ralph, call the preacher and cancel the wedding reservations, then tell the cook not to plan a reception." Behind him he could hear the pleased and triumphant murmurs of his family. "Call Captain Tolliver and tell him we want him to perform the ceremony on our way to Athens."

Luke hung up and turned back to his stunned family. "As I said, I don't need permission."

Luke and Caprice were married in international waters as the sun set in red, gold, and purple glory.

"I still can't believe it," she said as they stood at the rail and watched the brilliant sun disappear over the horizon. "Are we really married?"

"Yes, we really are. Do you regret not having a church wedding?"

"No, but I regret the reason. Is your family terribly upset?"

He smiled down at her and touched a bright tendril of hair that was being tossed about by the wind. "Yes."

"They won't ever accept me, will they?" she asked.

"In time they will. In my family everybody wants to be the chief and nobody wants to be the Indian. Except Winston, of course, and Christine has him pretty well trained already."

"That's sad."

"Winston's a big boy. He could stand up to her if he chose to."

"I don't want to come between you and your family. I never expected that."

"You aren't at fault. Besides, they'll come around in time. They were only opposed to our marriage because they don't know you."

"You should have listened to them, you know. You don't know me very well."

"Yes, I do. I know the part that counts."

He put his arm around her, and together they watched the last sliver of the sun disappear beneath the surface of the rippling sea. The amethyst-tinted water gradually darkened to an inky black, and the vivid colors of the sky paled as twilight settled over the sea. The evening star was followed by one, then clusters until more stars than she had ever seen dotted the night.

Luke watched her rapt expression as the yacht's lights illuminated their small world. Everything seemed to fill her with wonder, as if she had never seen or done any of it before.

"Are you ready to go below?" he asked.

Caprice nodded and looped her arm around his waist as they strolled across the deck. "Let's stay out here on the water forever," she suggested as she leaned her head back against his shoulder. "No one can touch us out here or hurt us or threaten us.'' She was thinking of what Katie had said about Caprice being foolish to sign the prenuptial agreement. Katie had scoffed that a man in love wouldn't have insisted she sign anything. Katie was changing, and Caprice felt as if she were a different person, too.

"No one can hurt you," Luke said.

"No? I feel as if I'm someone else these days, and I'm not sure who that person is."

"You're my love, just as I'm yours." They went down the steps and through the enclosed solarium, then down another flight to the main saloon. "Was there a problem with your sister? Something seemed to be bothering you before I told you about my family's objections."

Caprice glanced at him, then turned away again. She and Katie had rarely had such an argument. Katie had even accused Caprice of feathering her own nest and leaving Heather to die, because five thousand a month was chicken feed compared to two-hundred-thousand dollars. Caprice had managed to sell her Pontiac and after she bought the things she would need as Luke's wife, she had given the rest to Katie. Yet Katie actually seemed to begrudge her the amount she had held back for necessities. "No problem," she told Luke, not meeting his eyes.

They walked through the saloon and back toward the master suite. Luke turned on the stereo and the faint purr of the engines was gone.

Caprice stood amid the luxury of the room, wondering what to do next. A rare shyness gripped her as she watched him remove his coat and hang it in the closet, then pull the tie from his neck. He came to her and gazed down into her eyes. His skin was tan in sharp contrast to the open collar of his white shirt.

"You look as if you suddenly discovered you're Bluebeard's most recent wife," he teased. "I don't plan to ravish you and throw you to the sharks."

She smiled faintly. "I was thinking how inadequate I feel."

"Just close your eyes and think of England," he advised with a laugh. He lifted her chin and kissed her tenderly. "I love you, darling. Don't be afraid."

"I'm not afraid. I'm worried that I won't please you."

Luke smiled as he pulled her into his embrace. Caprice went willingly and his lips were warm upon hers and his breath sweet in her mouth. Churning excitement rose quickly in her as he ran his tongue over the softness of her lips and across the ridges of her teeth. She was his at last, with no more reasons to hold back.

Caprice kissed him with the urgent anxiety of not knowing if the marriage would last beyond their return to Houston. So much could go wrong between his family's disapproval and Katie's strange behavior. Caprice gave herself to Luke to blot out the tormenting thoughts.

His hand moved over her back and around to cup her breast. Caprice could feel the heat from his palm through the thin fabric of her dress and bra. She wanted more; she wanted to feel his flesh against hers, to become completely his.

She stepped back and slipped off her heels, then began undoing the row of pearl buttons down the front of her teal blue dress. She had bought it especially for this day, and she wasn't at all concerned that its quality might give her away.

"Let me," Luke said. His fingers nimbly unfastened the buttons to below her waist. Almost reverently he stroked the fabric from her shoulders and let it fall to the floor, pooling about her feet.

Caprice let him gaze at her as she lowered her half-slip and smoothed away the silken wisp of her pantyhose. She hesitated, knowing her new bra and silk bikini panties did very little to conceal her body. Slowly her shyness was replaced by confidence as she saw the expression of love on Luke's face and how his eyes followed her curves.

She unbuttoned his shirt as he reached around her to loosen his cuffs. She couldn't release his belt, so he removed the rest of his clothes. Caprice stared at him in unabashed fascination. She had known he was powerfully built, but she hadn't expected the pagan magnificence of his rippling muscles and lean strength. Nor had she ever seen a man in a state of arousal. Rather than being frightened, she found the sight of him inspired her to greater passion. "You're beautiful!" she murmured as she ran her hands over the knotted muscles on his stomach. "I never expected you to look like this!"

Luke reached behind her and unfastened the thin strap of her bra and pulled it away. Words failed him. Caprice was built like a goddess of love. Her full breasts lifted proudly, and the rosy nipples were tiny, pouting buds, eager to be touched and kissed. Her slender waist flowed smoothly into the roundness of her hips, and as he swept away her panties he noticed that the red-gold nest of curls below her waist was slightly darker than the cloud of hair that curled upon her shoulders. "Caprice," he whispered as if her name were an endearment.

"Do I please you?"

"Beyond my wildest dreams. I love you."

"I love you, too."

Luke reached past her to pull back the covers of the bed. As she lay down beside him on sheets that were as blue as a summer sky, she noticed that the mattress was as soft as thistledown. Possessively he drew her to him, and as their naked bodies touched, she reflexively drew in her breath. She had so much she wanted to say, but couldn't speak. Even had she been able to, there were no words that could express what she was feeling for him. For a while they lay still, absorbing all they could from the moment.

Slowly Luke drew his fingers over the fullness of her breast and gently rolled her nipple between his thumb and forefinger. Caprice's eyes darkened like a stormy sea as he caressed her, inciting an undeniable need for him. When he lowered his head and let his lips cover the beading rosette, she closed her eyes, marveling at this new sensation. Threading her fingers in his thick hair, she urged him to enjoy her completely.

Luke was trembling with desire for her, but he remembered that this was her first time, and he was determined that she would enjoy it, so he continued to suckle gently at her breasts as his hands kneaded and smoothed her supple skin. Instinctively she writhed against him, and as he let her know what pleased him, she responded by giving him more and telling him what pleased her.

Caprice could scarcely contain her excitement. It was as though all her muscles had turned to jelly, yet at the same time a primeval urgency hammered through her veins. The feel of his warm, firm skin beneath her hands and the barely leashed strength in his taut muscles were almost as stimulating as his lips and hands on her own body. With his gentle encouragement, she parted her legs and freely opened herself to him. His fingers stroked her secret curls, and then moved deeper to touch her as no man ever had before. The sensation shot through her like a bolt of lightning.

Caprice moaned and lifted her hips against his hand as her fingers explored his desire-swollen center. Luke said her name in a choked voice, and she reveled in his pleasure.

He held himself back by sheer force of will as she touched him intimately with an irresistible combination of innocence and seduction. As she moved beneath him in complete abandon, he slid between her thighs and gently entered her.

Caprice's eyes flew open and she tensed at the unexpected sensation. He gently reassured her, and in moments the minor discomfort was forgotten. She put her hands on the firm curve of his buttocks and drew him fully into her.

Luke was motionless until he felt he was in control and Caprice had become sufficiently accustomed to the feel of him deep within her. Then he began moving slowly, deeply, drawing passion from her depths and giving her all the love in his soul. Within moments she was moving with him, matching her thrusts to his. He knew she would need help to achieve her first completion because this was all so new to her, so he shifted slightly and put his fingers on the pulse of her desire.

Ecstasy rapidly grew within her, and as she moved against him, her passion built to a height she could not have imagined. His knowing fingers helped her over the brink to fulfillment, and she cried out softly as waves of pleasure thundered through her. She felt him push harder into her body as he reached his own peak, and she held him tightly as they flew on the wings of love.

Luke rolled slightly to one side to ease his weight off her, but not far enough to separate their bodies from the embrace. "I love you, Caprice."

"I know. You made it so wonderful for me. If I hadn't already loved you, I would have after tonight. Is it always this good when people make love?"

He smiled and caressed the apricot softness of her cheek with the back of his fingers. "It will be for us. This is only the beginning. In lovemaking, familiarity breeds contentment."

"And passion, and ecstasy, and delight, and fulfillment." She smiled at him and rested her hand on the rapid pulse in his neck. "We may see very little of Lisbon and Athens and all the rest. We may never leave this cabin." With a broader smile, she added, "I almost hope we don't."

"You'll have me every night and every day if that's what you want. I don't see how I'll ever be able to get enough of you."

"Just let me love you," she said softly. "That's all I ask."

"I'm so glad I found you."

The soft strains of music wrapped about them and the subtle movements of the boat cradled them as once again they began the dance of love.

They reached Lisbon within an hour of the time Captain Tolliver had predicted and moored offshore. The newlyweds spent the day in the city's teeming markets and sun-baked streets. Late that afternoon they weighed anchor, and by early the next morning they were in Cádiz. Caprice tried to resurrect her high-school Spanish to Luke's amusement and the Spaniards' confusion. Often her eyes were wide with wonder at the sights as she forgot to temper her awed expressions.

Another day and night of sailing took them to the island of Palma, where Luke had arranged for them to be included in the medieval dinner for which the island is famous. Afterward they were entertained by a realistic joust.

Caprice held Luke's hand as they strolled back through the balmy night to the *Idlewild*. "I never knew it could be like this."

"Marriage, you mean?"

"Marriage, travel, life—all of it."

Luke studied her in the dim light. "You've never been to Europe?"

Caprice caught her mistake and smiled disarmingly. "I've never eaten medieval food nor attended a joust."

He smiled but was more than a little puzzled by what sounded like naïveté. And in the Spanish marketplaces he had thought she was remarkably interested in everything—as if she had never seen any of it before. "There's a mystery about you," he said as if he were thinking aloud. "A part of you that eludes me."

"I'm only me," she replied with a shrug. More than anything she wanted to be able to tell him everything. Now that she knew him so well, she thought he might understand. She glanced at his handsome profile and recalled the sensuous pressure of his lips upon hers and how he pleased her night after night.

On the other hand, she could also see an iron strength in her husband, a ruthlessness masked by his gentle smile. She hadn't witnessed the scene between Luke and his family, but he had been able to override them all and even exclude them from the wedding. He was gentle, but he was certainly not soft.

What would she do if she told him the whole truth now, and he sailed away, abandoning her in this foreign country where she couldn't even speak the language? Was he capable of that? She shouldn't take the chance. For safety's sake, Caprice decided she should wait until after Heather's operation to bare her soul. This was no small secret she was hiding, and the blowup that was likely to occur might not be small either. No, she thought, it was much better to wait until they were home and settled into a comfortable routine.

"What are you thinking?" he asked.

"About you," she answered truthfully.

Late the next day they arrived in Nice, then skipped to Livorno by morning. Leaving the *Idlewild*, they journeyed inland to Pisa and from there to Florence. Caprice found the great cathedral so awe-inspiring that she almost dreaded leaving. Architecture that had been old before America had known the white settler's cabins humbled her.

They left Livorno that evening and sailed into Naples a little after noon. Mount Vesuvius towered beyond the congested coastline, and banks of clouds were building behind the volcano. Once more Luke noted Caprice's fascination with sights he had known since boyhood. More and more he was convinced that she had never seen any of these places before. Whenever he questioned her, she gave him one of her heart-stopping smiles and typically evasive answers. Luke was intrigued, but he never openly confronted her.

By the next morning they reached Messina on the isle of Sicily. The incredible array of flowers and the mountainous panorama made Caprice as excited as a girl on her first holiday. Luke found as much enjoyment in her reactions as he did in the places themselves. Before leaving he bought her one of the lace dresses for which Messina is known. She was as pleased as if she had never had such a gift before in her life.

Another day and night passed before the *Idlewild* reached Piraeus, the ancient port of Athens. Hand in hand they explored the ruins of the Acropolis, and as they walked the streets, they tried to imagine ancient Greeks walking before them.

Luke tried to buy her a dinner ring set with topaz and diamonds, but she insisted on one carved from coral.

"This one?" he asked. "It's rather plain, isn't it?"

"That's why I like it." She couldn't explain to him that she was becoming overwhelmed by her sudden immersion into a world of such riches. The coral ring was beautiful in its simplicity, even though its modest price made it affordable to everyone. Luke bought it for her, and while her back was turned he bought the topaz and diamond one, too.

Luke tried to buy her a fur jacket, but Caprice only laughed. "A fur? In this heat?"

"Athens has some of the best ones on the market."

"I don't want a fur coat."

"You don't?" He couldn't picture either Paulette or Christine hesitating.

"That's right, I really don't."

He took her hand as they strolled on the sunny pavement. "I like you, lady."

"I like you, too."

"I can't wait for Ralph to meet you."

"Why is that?"

Luke only smiled and hugged her.

That night on the *Idlewild*, Luke brought a tray of crackers and cheeses and wine to the master suite and they ate their supper curled up on the sky-blue sheets. Caprice fed Luke a bit of cheese and said, "Let's take all our honeymoons here."

"All of them?"

"I have a feeling every vacation with you will be a honeymoon."

"We haven't seen Britain yet, or Switzerland, or the fjords of Norway."

"No, I've never seen them. Are they wonderful?"

"Yes, they are." He put a wedge of cheese on a cracker and carried it to her lips. How could she not have traveled to the great sights of Europe? Luke had always loved a mystery, and he was thoroughly enjoying the discovery of Caprice. "Tomorrow we'll see Plaka, the old town. That's where they sell copperware and crafts. The taverns are a great place to hear *bazouki* music."

"I can hardly wait."

"Houston may seem dull by comparison when we go home."

"No it won't," she said, "because you will be there." She lifted a piece of cheese and saw a gleam of topaz atop it. "What...Luke! You bought that ring anyway."

"Our life will be full of surprises."

She wondered if he had any idea how prophetic his statement was.

Chapter Nine

Caprice was silent as she and Luke looped around the chrome and glass buildings of downtown Houston on their way home. During their month-long honeymoon, she had fallen deeply in love with Luke and now saw her scheme as a reprehensible act. Why, she fretted, hadn't she been straight with him? Luke was a very sensitive and generous man, and he might have simply given her the money for Heather's operation. But if he had, she would have gone her way, and he would have gone his, and she wouldn't have known the nights of loving in his strong and gentle embrace.

After so long at sea, the crush of traffic and the city's frantic pace made Caprice feel edgy and more than a little claustrophobic. When Luke finally exited onto Kirby Drive, her frayed nerves calmed somewhat. As they drove through the gate into River Oaks, a safe harbor from the storm of humanity that pressed all around them, her whole body relaxed.

"You're being awfully quiet," Luke said. "Are you tired?"

"A little. Yes, I am."

"You didn't seem very tired last night."

She smiled at him. The last official night of their honeymoon had been very, very special. "Maybe that's why I'm tired today."

"I get the feeling there's more to it than that." He turned down a quiet street. "Do you want to tell me about it?"

"Really, Luke, whatever could be wrong?" she asked in her best River Oaks accent.

"Why are you suddenly talking like Christine?"

Caprice sighed. He already knew her too well. Over the course of their honeymoon she had been unable to keep up her patina of glamour every minute. She imagined the problem he could more easily accept, and said, "If you must know, I'm worried about seeing your family."

"Don't let that bother you. As mad as they were when I last saw them, they won't speak to us for several more weeks. We'll worry about it then."

"That's easy for you to say. They love you. They will never accept me."

"Yes, they will."

"No, they won't."

"They will when they realize they have both of us or neither."

Caprice looked over at him and saw the stubborn line of his jaw. "I couldn't live with myself if I thought I had split up your family."

"Honey, if they love me, they'll want me to be happy. Right? I'm happier with you than I've ever been in all my life."

"You make it sound so simple."

"Most things are when you cut down to the core."

She wondered how he would find simplicity in their relationship if he knew the whole truth. At that point he might be more apt to agree with his family and toss her out. A chill passed through her. "I love you, Luke," she said to chase away the hobgoblins in her mind. "I really love you."

He laughed softly. "I really love you, too."

As they parked at the back of the house, a tall man in a dark suit came to meet them. "Who is he?" Caprice asked as the man came around to open her door.

"That's Lawford. Technically he's the butler, but he does a lot of other things as well."

"What butler? I never saw a butler here before!"

"He doesn't live in, and I usually let the staff go before dinnertime."

"Staff!" Caprice had no time to say more; Lawford opened her door and stood waiting for her to get out. She tried to comply with dignity.

Luke stood and over the top of the car said, "Caprice, this is Lawford. You'll be working through him the way I work through Ralph. He will see to it that the cook prepares whatever you want to have for dinner or parties."

She nodded to the stern man as she wondered where she would find the courage to tell him anything at all. When she turned, she found two women standing on the porch. The darker one she recognized from the first night she had come here.

"You remember Juanita," Luke said. "She's the housekeeper and prepares the meals when the cook is off for the day. Mrs. Thompson is the cook. She makes the best desserts you've ever tasted, and can handle any dinner parties that you might want to plan." He nodded to a man standing by the fence. "This is Pablo. He's Juanita's cousin, and he takes care of the lawns and gardens."

"It's nice to meet you all," Caprice said in what she hoped was a competent voice. She had never had even a part-time maid, and had no idea what to do with an entire staff.

"I'll prepare the suggested menu for the week by this afternoon, Mrs. Banning," the plump cook said. "Will that be soon enough?"

"Yes, that's fine." Caprice struggled to recall the correct name. Thompson, that was it. "That will be fine, Mrs. Thompson."

Lawford got the bags out of the car as Luke and Caprice went past the kitchen door to enter the house through a side door. When she looked back, the staff had disappeared. Even the luggage was out of sight.

"You never mentioned a staff," she said almost accusingly to Luke.

"I assumed you knew there would be one. With a house this size, how else could I manage?"

How indeed, she thought, as she considered the rambling structure. Cleaning this enormous hacienda would take her entire day, and she suspected the kitchen would look like a chef's dream of high-tech heaven. The thought of cooking for Luke's family sent a chill through her, and she was especially thankful for the reassuring competence of Mrs. Thompson and Juanita.

They crossed a sun room with its jungle of potted plants and wicker hanging chairs, then went through a formal dining room Caprice had never seen. As in the living room, the colors were those of a sun-washed desert, but here the effect was pure elegance.

Instead of turning toward the living room, Luke led her down a quarry-tiled hall. "You may as well meet Redoubtable Ralph," he said.

Caprice nodded. She wanted to get all the introductions over with so she wouldn't have any left to dread. More than ever before she felt like an imposter. She was more qualified to be the hired help in a place like this than to be the mistress.

"Ralph," Luke said as he opened the office door, "here she is!" He presented his new bride as if she were royalty. "Caprice, this is Ralph Slayton. He's the one who keeps me on time for appointments and makes sure there are appointments to keep."

Caprice saw a thin, ascetic man with thick glasses, thinning black hair, and very pale skin. He wasn't smiling. "Hello, Mr. Slayton," she said with forced cordiality as she held out her hand.

"You may call me Ralph," he said as he shook her fingertips. "I hope you had a pleasant voyage." He didn't look as if he meant anything of the kind.

"Yes," Caprice said as she withdrew her hand. "We did." She didn't like this man, and she could tell he didn't like her either.

Luke beamed at Caprice as if he still couldn't believe his good fortune. "Didn't I tell you that she's perfect?"

"Yes, I believe you mentioned that, frequently."

"Don't pay any attention to him," Luke said as he saw Caprice's face pale. "Ralph always talks like that. Did the contracts arrive from Yaron?"

"Yes." From a nearby file, Ralph extracted a document of some sort. "If you want to sign it now, I can get it back to him in the next mail." Looking straight at Caprice, Ralph added, "I tried to push the deal through before the wedding, but found it impossible."

Luke took a pen from the neat assortment on the desk and signed the contract. "That was easy enough." He poked the pen back into the leather holder and casually said, "That makes us two million dollars richer."

Caprice's eyes widened involuntarily. When she glanced at Ralph, she found him intently watching her. *He knows*, she thought nervously.

"Did you get the keys made?" Luke asked his manager.

"Yes." Ralph reached into the lap drawer of the desk and took out several keys with neatly printed tags.

"What are these for?" Caprice asked when Ralph handed them to her.

Luke went through them one by one. "This unlocks the house. Put this one in the burglar alarm as soon as you come inside—I'll show you how to do it. This one belongs to the Maserati. I know how much you like cabs, but I think we should buy you a car of your own. Think it over and decide what kind you want."

"A car?" she asked softly. She stared down at the keys in her palm.

Luke took a pen and jotted down a series of numbers on a notepad. "This is the combination of the safe. I'll show you where it is. Memorize the numbers. No one is allowed to know it except the three of us."

"Luke," Ralph said in a tight voice. "Are you sure that's necessary? There's really no need for..."

"Caprice is my wife, Ralph." Luke's voice held a clipped warning, and Caprice realized he had been aware all along of Ralph's antagonism toward her. "Surely you aren't suggesting she shouldn't be allowed access to the safe."

"No. Of course not." Ralph drew back and looked coolly from one to the other.

"I didn't think so." Luke smiled and said, "How about a swim, Caprice?"

"I'm afraid it will have to wait," Ralph said. "I took the liberty of setting up a meeting with Mr. Allerbee this afternoon."

"Today? I just got home."

"If you'll recall, you were due back yesterday."

Luke frowned. "I guess I'd better not cancel it. Allerbee isn't a pleasant person when he has to change his plans." To Caprice he said, "I'm sorry, honey. Allerbee's office is all the way downtown. I won't be home until dinnertime."

"That's all right," she said quickly. "It will give me a chance to unpack and rest."

"Lawford will have already taken care of our luggage," Luke said.

"Oh."

"Come on and I'll show you the rest of the house. Ralph, if she needs anything, you take care of it. Right?" He formed it as a question, but it was clearly a command.

"Right. I've opened the account in her name, by the way. She needs to sign this card and I can finish the paperwork."

"What account?" Caprice asked.

"Your monthly allowance," Ralph said coolly. "Surely you haven't forgotten."

Luke gave him a level stare as Caprice wrote her name on the signature card. When she was finished, he reached in his pocket and handed her several one hundred dollar bills. Ralph looked as if he would like to object, but he said nothing. Caprice took the money.

"That should hold you until Ralph sets you up at the bank. Go shopping while I'm gone. We have cards at Neiman's, Joske's, Foley's, and some others." He handed her the cards he mentioned. "If you want to open other accounts, go ahead."

"You're so generous," she said in a low voice.

"As my wife, you're entitled to all my privileges."

Caprice was all too aware of Ralph's displeasure, and she knew Luke was doing this in front of him so Ralph would know how things stood. She dared a glance at Ralph and found him glaring at her as if she were a snake. There had been others whom she had disliked on sight, just as there was Luke, whom she had liked immediately. She couldn't explain the phenomenon, but she wished Ralph were not so dislikable, and that it wasn't so obviously mutual.

She was glad to leave the manager's office and complete the tour of the house.

The master bedroom was at the end of the other wing, past the game room and library. The decor of desert tones and sunny blues was continued, along with the adobe walls. The carpet was the color of golden sand and the bedroom ceiling was paneled in narrow oak strips. A kiva fireplace was on one wall and the greenhouse windows on the other overlooked the pool. As Luke had said, the butler had already seen to it that Caprice's bags were unpacked and put out of sight.

Luke went to one of the two large walk-in closets and opened the door. Caprice's few clothes looked out of place in the vast space that was nearly as big as Heather's bedroom.

"This is odd," he said. "I had assumed your other things would have been delivered by now. Didn't your sister know where to send them?"

"I travel light," Caprice said quickly. "I don't like having to keep up with a lot of things."

"I know, but ... wait a minute, are you saying this is all you own?"

She wet her lips nervously and shrugged.

"Caprice, nobody owns this few clothes. Why, these are only the things you took on our honeymoon."

Which story, she considered, would he be most likely to believe? A fire? A burglary? "When I moved back to Houston, I got rid of everything I didn't especially want. I always do that. I guess I just don't like to pack."

His look suggested he couldn't quite believe what he was hearing. "*All* of it? Even your winter clothes and furs?"

"Well, not *all* of it exactly," she hedged with a short laugh. "Some of it I loaned to my sister. There was ... a fire. She lost quite a few of her things."

"That's why you moved in with her?"

"Yes, she needed my help. Luckily for her, we're about the same size."

"What about insurance? Surely she didn't lose everything!"

"Not everything, but her clothes were damaged, and she is having problems getting the insurance company to pay off."

"When was this? What caused the fire?"

"Oh, Luke, I really don't want to talk about it. She's all right now, and ..."

"Go shopping and get whatever you need. You should make a fresh start." He closed her closet door. "Better yet, I'll go with you."

"You will?" She could see her entire month's allowance dwindling. Katie needed that money more than Caprice needed clothes. Especially since this marriage was likely to be short-lived.

"I want to help pick out what you need. We'll go tomorrow."

"My bank account may not be active by then."

"Ralph will take care of that this afternoon, but we won't use that. The monthly allowance is only to keep Ralph happy. I'll sign the charge slips and the money will come out of the household account."

Caprice didn't know what to say. This was the man she had intended to use to get money. She felt terribly guilty. "Thank you, Luke."

"No need to thank me. I love you." He glanced at his watch and crossed the room to kiss her goodbye. "I need to go if I'm going to get to that appointment on time."

She closed her eyes and held him, enjoying his warm scent and the strength of his arms about her. "Drive carefully," she said as she lifted her face to kiss him.

"It's hard to leave you, even for a few hours."

"I know," she whispered. "I feel the same way about you."

"I'll be back by dinnertime." He kissed her again, his lips lingering on hers.

She watched him go. The room felt empty without his magnetic presence. She sat on the edge of the wide bed as she looked around the room. For the first time she wondered what she was supposed to do to fill her days. Leisure time was a luxury she had rarely experienced.

When she dialed Katie's number, a recording informed her the number she had reached was no longer in service. Her blood ran cold. Had something happened to them while she was gone? Had Heather's condition suddenly worsened? Without another thought, she called for a cab.

Within the hour she stood on Katie's familiar front walk. For a minute she stared at the house, as if she were seeing it with new eyes. The paint was peeling on the windowsills and looked dingy in the sunlight. The roof sagged as though it needed repair, or replacement. As Katie had no penchant for gardening, only a few straggly bushes flanked the house. Caprice had spent all her efforts on the vegetable garden in back, and the front lawn looked as neglected as most of its neighbors.

She went up onto the cracked slab that served as a front porch and hesitated before opening the weather-stained door. She had a sudden feeling of vertigo. It was as if this house belonged to a previous life.

Heather was watching a game show on television, and when she saw Caprice, she rolled off the sagging couch and ran to her. "Mom! Mom! Aunt Cappy's here!"

Caprice smiled with relief that things seemed to be no worse than when she had left town, but when she hugged her niece, she was dismayed to notice that Heather felt much thinner, and that she was still running a low-grade fever. As she held her at arm's length to look at her, she could see that her skin was sallower, her blond hair was lusterless, and her eyes were sunken.

Katie came in from the kitchen, bringing with her the pungent odors of steaming cabbage and onions.

She wiped her palms on her checkered apron before hugging Caprice. "Sit down and tell me all about it," Katie said as she shoved her hair back from her sweat-dampened forehead.

"You can't imagine how beautiful it was," Caprice began, then faltered because she knew Katie really couldn't. How could she explain the cathedral in Florence to someone who had a dishpan on the floor to catch drips from the next rain? How could she describe a medieval feast on Palma when cabbage was the most expensive thing cooking in the kitchen? "Italy was my favorite. It's so wonderful and the people were so friendly."

"Yes, yes, but did you get the money?" Katie asked eagerly.

After an awkward pause, Caprice said, "Not yet."

Katie's eyes grew troubled, but she said, "I guess it is a bit soon. I just thought after a whole month..."

"I tried to call, but your phone doesn't seem to be working," Caprice said.

"It's been disconnected. Heather was in the hospital for a couple of days with another secondary infection. I didn't have enough money to pay the phone bill."

"Heather, are you feeling better now?" Caprice asked in concern.

"I'm okay." The girl went back to the couch and flopped down to watch the game show.

Caprice pulled out the money Luke had given her, kept fifty dollars, and gave the rest to Katie. She tried not to notice that Katie's eyes followed the fifty back into her purse. "I'll send you a check for four thousand as soon as my account is active."

"Four? I thought your allowance was five thousand."

"It is, but I can't give you the entire amount. I may need something. How could I explain not having any cash?"

"A thousand dollars for spending money?"

"Katie, I'm expected to always have more than enough."

"I guess you're right," Katie said, her lips tight. "Anyway, it's your money."

"Katie! How can you say that to me?"

"Oh, yeah, I forgot what a sacrifice you're making for us. You tell me about Italy, and I'll tell you about not being able to pay the phone bill."

"That's not fair," Caprice retorted, glaring at her sister.

Katie shrugged. "When has life ever been fair? Are you staying for supper? We're having soup."

"No, thanks. Luke will be expecting me. Use this to get some meat. I think Heather is losing weight."

Katie looked over at her daughter. "Come into the kitchen with me, Caprice."

They went through the small rooms, and Caprice sat on a kitchen chair as Katie stirred the soup on the stove.

Caprice sighed heavily. "Well? Why are you acting like your nose is out of joint?"

"Heather is sinking faster than the doctor first thought. He's trying another new medication, but she doesn't seem to be responding." Katie drew a deep breath. "He says she may not . . . be here next year for sure."

Caprice's heart ached, and she found it difficult to breathe. "We'll get the money, Katie. Look how far we've come already."

"Have we?" Katie demanded bitterly. "I see how far *you've* come, but four thousand dollars isn't much when we need two hundred thousand! We won't even have enough for the down payment within a year at this rate. If Heather lasts that long."

"I'm doing my best!" Caprice said. "What do you expect? That's a lot of money. I can't just walk up to Ralph Slayton and demand that much money."

"You said you could when you thought up this scheme!"

"Things aren't the way I thought they would be. They don't throw money around the way we thought. That's a lot of money whether your name is Dolan *or* Banning!"

"It's a hell of a lot if your name is Farnell," Katie retorted. "And we're counting on you. We banked everything on this gamble!"

"Katie, I'm telling you, the money will be there."

"Maybe. Maybe not. I don't know how long Heather can hang on. At least you got a millionaire and a trip to Italy."

Caprice gasped at the bitterness in Katie's voice. She could understand her sister's jealousy, and certainly her worry over Heather, but Katie seemed to resent Caprice as much as she resented everyone in River Oaks. Had Katie changed or had Caprice never seen this side of her before?

As if she knew what Caprice was thinking, Katie jabbed the wooden spoon into the simmering pot. "I'm trying to accept things the same way I always did before, but Heather's life is at stake. I have to sit around here knowing I can't do one damned thing but wait on Mrs. Luke Banning. And when she finally comes home, all she has is a promise that she'll somehow come through in time. It's as though I was given hope and then had it snatched away. What if we go through all this and Heather dies?" The words "and you're still Mrs. Luke Banning" hung unspoken between them.

"That won't happen."

"No?" Katie shoved tears away with the heel of her hand. "So how's your millionaire?"

Caprice paused. "I love him, Katie. I really do."

Katie gave a snorting laugh. "That couldn't be too difficult. I guess I could manage to love a millionaire, too."

"That's not why I love him. He's gentle and sensitive and . . ."

"So was Jed at first. After a few months they all revert back to the bastards they really are."

Caprice stood up. "I have to go. I told the cab driver to pick me up in half an hour. That must be him honking now."

"Half an hour? That's not much of a visit. But then I guess you have more to look forward to these days than cabbage soup and TV."

"Quit it, Katie. This is me you're talking to."

Katie looked over at her, and Caprice saw her chin quiver. "I'm sorry," Katie said at last. "I know I shouldn't be jealous, but I can't help it. All my life you were the one who did best in school and got the best job. Now look at you." Tears welled in her eyes, but she pushed them back and managed a wavery smile. "I'm trying, Cappy. I really am."

Caprice hugged her sister. "Turn off that soup and go get yourselves a solid meal. We're going to get the money some way."

"Cabbage isn't as good the second day. I'll buy meat tomorrow when I get the phone turned back on." She returned Caprice's hug. "Run along. That cab won't wait forever, and you can't call another one from here."

Caprice hurried out, dropping a kiss on Heather's cheek as she passed. She was still upset over Katie's attitude, but she couldn't change it. She was so upset she didn't notice the tan car that had followed her to the house, nor that the car followed her to within sight of her new home.

The man driving the nondescript car was as physically unobtrusive as his vehicle. Even if Caprice had noticed him, she would never have given him a second glance. His unremarkable appearance was one reason Morris Ainsley was so successful as a private investigator.

Chapter Ten

As the cab pulled away from Caprice's new home and she walked toward the front door, she couldn't help but compare her surroundings with Katie's house. Although she hadn't noticed it before, the small house had become quite run-down. Jed had never been good at home repairs, and now that he was gone and Katie didn't have the money to pay for such services, most of the work had been left undone. Katie kept the house spotlessly clean, but that didn't repair the roof, patch the cracked front porch, or replace the sagging couch.

Caprice let herself into the house and looked about the posh interior. She had so much and Katie had so little. She understood her sister's jealousy all too well.

She went to the master bedroom and closed the door behind her. Beyond the glass wall was the pool in its serene splendor; the tall banana trees were reflected in the placid water. Beneath her feet the sand-colored carpet was soft and plush. This was a far cry indeed from Katie's little house in the Heights. She thought how much Heather would enjoy swimming in that pool, and she wondered if it would ever be possible.

As she turned back to the room, she noticed a small gift box on the bed. There was no note with the box or any other indication of its intended recipient. For a moment she considered waiting to ask Luke about the box, but her curiosity got the better of her. When she lifted the lid, she found a strand of creamy pearls, coiled on a bed of velvet. As she withdrew them, she recognized the store name printed on the satin interior as the one from which Luke had bought her wedding rings. She draped the pearls around her neck and looked in the mirror. Only slightly lighter than her skin, the pearls seemed to glow with pale translucence.

Hearing a sound at the door, she turned to find Luke standing there. He smiled and said, "I see you found the pearls."

"Yes, but why..."

"Every woman needs pearls. I've heard Christine say so a dozen times. On our way back from the Mediterranean, I called Ralph and asked him to get them for you. Do you like them?"

"Of course I do. But I have nothing to wear them with."

"You will have. We're going shopping tomorrow, remember?"

"I wasn't asking for more. Luke, you've been more than generous already. I don't need anything else."

"Yes, you do. You can't live in half a dozen dresses, you know." He went into the bathroom, and Caprice heard him turn on the faucet.

Slowly she removed the pearls and let them coil back into the velvet box. She didn't know what pearls cost, but she knew these were expensive. On top of that, Luke seemed determined to buy her a wardrobe.

Guilt assailed her. This had gone far enough. She had to tell him the truth. Because he was such a generous man, she was sure he would give her the money for Heather's operation, despite what she had been trying to do. Caprice hated to lie even about small things, and this huge deception had greatly disturbed her from the very beginning. When she had suggested it to Katie as a way to solve their problem, she hadn't expected it to work out like this. She had thought she and Luke would get to know each other and somehow she could talk him into giving her the money. She had never counted on falling in love.

She closed the box and looked through the doorway into the bathroom where Luke was combing his hair as he whistled a soft tune. She loved him so much. Not because of his money, but because of who he was. He was everything she had ever hoped to find in a man, and she knew he loved her, too. The only decent thing for her to do was to make a clean sweep and tell him everything.

"Luke?" she said in a rush. "I need to talk to you."

"Sure, honey. What is it?" He put down the comb and came into the bedroom as he removed his tie. "It's miserably hot out there. Want to go for a swim?"

"Not now." She wasn't at all sure how to bring up the subject. "You came home early. I didn't expect you until dinner."

He nodded as he unbuttoned his shirt. "It doesn't take long to fire a man." He sat on the bed to remove his shoes. "Caprice, I can't believe what happened. For months now I've known there was a problem with our company in Saint-Tropez. Someone was embezzling funds, but I wasn't sure who it was. I made a couple of trips over there, but the records had been doctored so skillfully that it looked as if three people could be at fault."

She sat beside him. "You look troubled. Did you lose much money?"

"Most of it was recovered. That's what Allerbee wanted to see me about. What really upsets me is who they found with his hand in the till."

"Who?"

"You wouldn't know him. His name is Fred Baker. He had actually rigged it so that three innocent people would carry the blame. They could have been fired or even sent to prison! In fact there were plans to arrest them as soon as all the facts were verified."

He looked over at her, and his eyes were filled with hurt and puzzlement. "Caprice, I trusted him. I was the one who hired Fred for the job, and I always felt he was completely honest. We've visited each other's homes. He even asked me to be his son's godfather!"

"Maybe there's some mistake," Caprice said softly. Luke's voice was tinged with bitter disappointment, although he was clearly trying to remain emotionally detached.

"No, I had hoped there would be, but there wasn't. He was caught forging a check and admitted everything."

"Maybe he needed the money."

"No way. He was being paid a handsome salary. No, the thing I can't stand is that he *lied* to me. He actually lied!" Luke stood and went to a drawer to get his swimsuit.

Caprice watched as he put it on. She felt cold all over. "There could have been a reason. Something he couldn't tell you."

"I guess that's my Achilles' heel. I can forgive anything except lies, and Fred knew it. I could forgive him doing anything at all but this. Even if someone kicked me in the face, I could forgive him more easily than if he lied to me." He turned to look back at her. "What did you want to talk to me about?"

Caprice's mouth felt as though it were full of cotton. "I . . . I wanted to say I love you."

Luke smiled, and the tension left his face. He stepped over to her and pulled her into his warm embrace. "I love you, darling. All through that meeting I kept thinking about you and how good it is to have someone I'm sure I can trust. The world may be full of Freds, but I have you."

She gripped him tightly. "What will happen to him?"

"I insisted that he only be fired. We got back most of the money, but even with the betrayal, I don't feel right about pressing charges against him. The prisons in southern France are hellholes. I couldn't do that to Fred." His voice became tighter as he added, "But I'll see to it that he never works for me again. I won't set out to destroy him, but if anyone asks for a reference, I'll tell them exactly what happened."

Caprice closed her eyes, and as she held on to him, she felt a slight tremble ripple through his body. He was still terribly upset. If he could get this angry over a man in Saint-Tropez, what would he say about her, the greatest liar of them all? No, she couldn't tell him the truth now. At least not until Heather was restored to health. Perhaps then she could gamble on being able to convince him that she had done it for a good cause. She wondered if that would matter.

"Come for a swim with me," he asked again. "I need to do something to relax."

"You go ahead. I'll be out in a minute."

He headed out the door leading to the pool and dove into the still water, barely disturbing its surface. Soon he was swimming with long, strong strokes that she knew would work away most of his anger. But what about his hurt? She loved him too much to tell him the truth. If she admitted that she had lied, he might never believe that her profession of love for him was the truth. And she knew him well enough to know that his wounds would be deep, and the scars would last forever.

* * *

Caprice had never shopped, or even dreamed of shopping, the way Luke did. They started at Neiman's, at one end of the Galleria, and worked their way to Doneby's, with a break for lunch at the Magic Pan. When the jeweler at Doneby's presented an exquisite necklace and matching bracelet of diamonds and emeralds, she panicked, her heart jumping to her throat.

"Luke," she whispered, "it's too much!"

"No, it isn't. And it matches your wedding ring perfectly." He nodded briefly, indicating that the man should wrap it up.

Caprice caught Luke's sleeve. "I can't let you spend so much money!"

"Honey, what else can you do with it? Since you gave your clothes to your sister, you really need these things. That necklace and earrings will be perfect with the white dress from Neiman's. Now, what about the pearls? Maybe we should look for a dress to—"

"My pearls will go with all the others. I refuse to get another one. Why, we just bought a whole wardrobe!"

"It's a beginning. You know, I still can't get over the way you worry about shopping. I thought all women loved to shop. I know, I'll ask Christine to let you know before she goes to Swayse's again. It's one of her favorite places."

"No! I mean, I don't like Swayse's style." She knew Mrs. Swayse would recognize her immediately. "I prefer Neiman's."

"Okay." He took the package from the jeweler and signed the ticket.

They went back into the busy mall and strolled by the railing to look down at the ice rink. "Do you skate?" he asked.

"I used to have roller skates when I was a child."

"If you can do one, you can do the other. We'll go sometime. How about skiing?"

"On water?"

"On snow."

"I've never tried."

"Not ever?" he asked in surprise.

"I'm not very athletic by nature," she said hastily.

"This Christmas, let's go to the Alps."

"What?"

"If you're going to learn to ski, you might as well do it in Switzerland. I have a chalet there and even if you don't take to the slopes, the view is incredible."

"You own a Swiss chalet?"

"Yes, but it's nothing like the one Christine and Winston are considering buying. Theirs looks like a palace. Ours was originally a hunting lodge. The caretakers keep it in good repair and have maintained it pretty much the way it was fifty years ago."

"You actually own a Swiss chalet," she repeated.

"*We* own it. Would you like to spend Christmas there? Maybe there's somewhere else you'd rather go?"

"No, no. That sounds wonderful." Christmas was more than three months away. By then, the marriage might be all over. She thought of telling Katie about this proposed trip, but she was reluctant even to think about it. Because of Katie's embittered attitude, Caprice was afraid this would make things worse.

"One more stop," Luke said as he guided her back into Neiman's.

"Not more clothes," she said firmly.

"I have something else in mind."

They took the escalator up to the fur salon. Caprice hung back. "Luke, it's ninety degrees outside!"

"It won't be forever. This is September. By next month you'll need a coat."

"I have a coat."

"No, you don't. I looked before we left the house. I find it amazing that you would give your sister all your clothes."

"As I said before, we're the same size, and there was a problem with her insurance company."

"Christine had the same trouble when she was robbed a few years back. The insurance companies seem to think we shop at bargain basements."

Caprice glanced at him. Until a month ago, she had.

Luke nodded to a saleswoman and said, "My wife would like to see a fur."

"Yes, ma'am. What did you have in mind?"

Caprice was at a loss for words. She had never tried on a fur coat in her life. "Perhaps a jacket," she stammered.

"How about this one?" Luke said, looking critically at a full-length mink. "It looks warm."

The saleslady pursed her carmine lips in an indulgent smile. "No, no, Mr. Banning. That color would be entirely wrong for her."

"You know us?" Caprice was startled into asking.

"We keep up with all our regulars, Mrs. Banning."
She went to another rack and drew out a silver fox
coat. "This would be much better with her coloring
than the dark one." She unlocked the restraining
cords.

Caprice tried on the coat and stared at herself in the
mirror. She had never felt anything more luxurious,
even though she was opposed to the idea of using real
animal fur for coats.

"It's too silvery," Luke objected.

"You're right. It's much too old for her." The
woman studied Caprice's pale red-gold hair. "I think
I have just the thing."

With a flourish she brought out a mink in a shade a
bit darker than Caprice's hair. Caprice put it on and
stepped before the mirror.

"I like that one," Luke said.

"So do I," chimed the saleslady. "It's perfect on
her. Now, she mentioned a jacket? Look at these.
They would be adorable for more casual wear."

Caprice tried on a snowy jacket that the lady assured her would go with anything from jeans to evening trousers. Thinking of her worn and faded jeans
at Katie's house, Caprice laughed.

"We'll take this one, too," Luke said.

"Both?" Caprice gasped.

"I'll write up the ticket," the saleslady cooed.
"Mrs. Banning is certainly a fortunate woman."

"Thank you," Caprice murmured. She felt as if she
were in shock. She was afraid even to look at the price
the woman was marking on the pad, and when she
did, she felt faint.

Luke was all for going to the shoe department, but Caprice caught his arm. "No more," she said. "I mean it, Luke."

"You're tired, aren't you," he said contritely. "I should have noticed that before now."

"Can we go home?"

"Sure." He took her hand, and they went out to the parking lot. The summer heat had refused to leave Houston, but a cool front had tempered things somewhat. It was no longer painfully hot.

"Do you know what I would like?" Caprice said as they entered the traffic snarl on Westheimer.

"What?"

"A hamburger. An old-fashioned gooey one from a fast food place. And a strawberry malt."

"It's yours. How about this place coming up?"

Caprice smiled at the sight of the familiar logo. "Perfect."

They ate at a slick-topped table and used paper napkins. For the first time in months, Caprice felt completely relaxed as she ate.

"You constantly amaze me," Luke said. "I would swear you're enjoying that greasy hamburger more than crepes at the Magic Pan."

"I like hamburgers," she said. "Don't you?"

"We're a lot alike. The longer I know you, the more I realize it. I do like hamburgers. The gooier the better."

"Can Mrs. Thompson cook everyday food?"

"Like a dream. That's why I hired her."

"Then why have we had only things like crepes and eggs Benedict?"

"I guess she's trying to impress you. All you have to do is to present her with a week's menu. She will cook whatever you ask."

"Oh. I thought she was supposed to bring me the menu, and I was to okay it."

"Either way."

Score one for the cook, Caprice thought. She made a mental note to change the elaborate menu Mrs. Thompson had presented to her that morning. Caprice hadn't admitted it, but she wasn't sure what some of the proposed dishes were. "I think we'll have chili dogs tomorrow night."

"Whatever turns you on," he said.

"You turn me on," she countered.

"Let's get out of here."

As they drove home they held hands, and when they breezed through the front door, Luke blithely avoided Ralph's message by way of the butler to go to the study to discuss a merger.

"Shouldn't you see about that?" she asked as they neared their room.

"Ralph can wait. I have a merger of my own in mind."

"Now?"

"Right now." He took her in his arms and closed the world out. "I've wanted to do this all day. Holding you like this satisfies some deep part of me."

"Me too." She breathed in the subtle aroma of his after-shave and clothing and the fresh smell of his skin. "I feel as if I'm at home when you hold me."

"In some ways you seem so untouched, so naïve. You seemed almost overwhelmed by our shopping trip, but you must have done that hundreds of times before. You always seem to be seeing things as if for the first time. It's so refreshing. I love that in you."

"You do?"

"I feel as if I'm showing you my world, and that it's a world you've never seen before. I know that sounds silly."

"No, it doesn't. I wasn't alive before I met you. Everything seems new to me. Everything."

He bent his head and kissed her long and slowly. Caprice held him tightly and let her world spin and narrow to enclose only the two of them.

"I love you, Luke," she murmured when he pressed her close and nuzzled the soft cloud of her hair.

"I never knew I could love anyone the way I love you. Caprice, you've given me so much!"

"I have?" She looked up at him in surprise.

"You've given me things I never found anywhere else. You seem to love me only for myself and not for what I can give you. That's a rare gift for someone in my position."

"At times I wish you didn't have a penny so I could show you that my love would be the same. I do love you for yourself, Luke. Never, never doubt that."

"When I look in your eyes, I see love shining there. I trust you as I've never trusted anyone."

"But you hardly know me," she murmured.

"I know you as well as if we had spent lifetimes together."

"I'll never intentionally hurt you, Luke." On the surface, this husband of hers might be self-assured and confident, but Caprice could see the part of his complex personality that no one else was shown. His wealth made him vulnerable; he lived every moment with the uncertainty of whether he was loved for himself or for his money.

As he led her to the bed, she said, "If there is ever a time when you doubt my love, or if something happens that makes me seem...false, please remember my love for you."

"You? False? Impossible. There isn't an ounce of duplicity in you." He smiled at her as he began unfastening her blouse. "I trust you completely."

She didn't answer. She wanted his trust and she wanted to deserve it. Desperately she tried to console herself with the reassurance that once Heather was taken care of, she would never betray him again. Only her fear for Heather prevented her from telling him now.

After they had undressed each other, Caprice drew back the bedcovers and stretched out on the silken sheets. Her bright hair made a crown about her face, and the apricot sheets cast a warm glow onto her skin.

Luke lowered himself beside her, and ran his hand lovingly over the curves and valleys of her pliant body. "You're so beautiful." Even though he spoke softly, his voice was deeply resonant. "And so responsive," he said as he watched her nipple bead to hardness with his touch.

"It's because I love you." She drew him to her and proved her love with kisses that left him breathless.

He enjoyed the warmth of her skin and the way her breasts filled the cupped palms of his hands. Her silken legs entwined with his, drawing him closer, and she moved against him with supple grace.

Luke drew one rosy nipple into his mouth, then turned to the other. Caprice was eager for him already, but he held back, urging them both to greater desire.

Her hands moved over him, touching him in the ways she knew would please him. That was the hallmark of their loving, he thought. Each tried to please the other more than themselves. The result was more incredible than anything Luke had known could exist between a man and a woman.

He ran his tongue over Caprice's silken skin and enjoyed the fine texture of her neck and breasts. "You taste good," he murmured.

She laughed softly, then he felt her tongue slide tantalizingly over his shoulder in a series of gentle circles. "You taste good, too."

She put her palms on his buttocks and slid lower to guide him into her. Luke strained to hold back as the stimulation of being enclosed within the core of her body threatened to overwhelm him. In a moment he opened his eyes to find her watching him in pleased amusement, and he knew that she was aware of the difficulty he was having.

Once she was satisfied that he was ready, she began to move, drawing out their pleasure to an exquisite degree. Luke let her take the lead and matched his strokes to hers. Her eyes darkened from sea-green to deep emerald. He fondled her breast and rolled her nipple between his thumb and forefinger, sending wave after wave of increasing pleasure through her until she thought she could bear no more. At last, her eyes closed tightly as a rapturous tidal wave engulfed her with the intense bliss she had come to expect from his masterful loving.

When her breathing became less ragged, Luke began moving inside her again, once more teasing her to heights of ecstasy. She writhed against him in eagerness to have all of him. Their lips met as they reached the peak together, and his tongue probed her mouth as pleasure roared through them both.

For a long time they lay linked together in love. Caprice heard Luke's steady breathing and felt the warm stirring of his breath in her hair. She loved him so much she ached from the intensity of it, even though he had sated her body's needs.

She closed her eyes and held him close as she thought how tenuous her happiness was. Along with Luke's vulnerable side was one of iron that had been forged to protect him from hurt. What if he threw her out of his life when he learned she was living a lie? He must never know! But if he wasn't told about Heather, how could she ever get the money? Her gaze traveled about the room and a daring plan began to form.

Chapter Eleven

Caprice drove Luke's Maserati to the Galleria, enjoying the sensation of being once again behind a steering wheel, especially such a luxurious one. This perfectly tuned sports car was a far cry from the aging vehicle she had sold to buy her trousseau, and she was reluctant to reach her destination.

She parked at the far corner of the lot for fear someone would scrape the car, then took the packages from the back seat. Clutching them tightly, she hurried across the parking lot. When she reached Neiman's fur salon, she sought out the saleslady who had sold her the coat and jacket. "I want to return these."

The lady gave her an uncertain look and opened the boxes. "Why, these are the furs you bought last week."

"That's right. As you can see, they haven't been out of the boxes."

"But why? Is there some flaw in them?"

"No, no. I just want to return them."

"Mrs. Banning, if something is wrong with them, I'll be happy to exchange them for you."

"I don't want an exchange. I want to return them and get a refund."

"But . . ."

Caprice drew herself up and fixed the woman with a regal glare. "Surely there is no problem here? I've never had trouble returning things to Foley's or Sakowitz. Will it be necessary for me to call my husband to see that this gets taken care of to my satisfaction?"

"No," the saleslady said hastily. "No, of course there is no problem. I was merely surprised." She looked over the sales ticket for a moment and said, "Since this was paid for by debit card, I'll have to have our office issue a check for the refund."

"Yes, of course. I've already filled out a deposit slip. If you'll attach it to your refund papers, your office can send the check directly to my bank."

"Mrs. Banning, this is a bit irregular. We normally—"

"You're not suggesting that I'm eccentric, are you? I'm sure Mr. Banning wouldn't want to hear—"

"Please, no. Of course not. How you handle things is entirely your business. I'll be happy to take care of this just as you wish. I'm certain that Mr. Banning is a busy man. We needn't bother him.''

Caprice smiled broadly, hoping the woman couldn't see the relief on her face as she took Caprice's bank deposit slip and began doing the necessary paperwork.

Next Caprice went to the jewelry store and lay both the box containing the diamond and emerald set and the box with the pearls on the counter. When the distinguished-looking salesman approached her, she said, ''I want to return these, please.''

He snapped open the boxes and frowned. ''Return them?''

''Yes. My name is Caprice Banning. My husband bought them for me and I would like to return them.''

The man looked at her strangely and said, ''Excuse me.'' He took the boxes of jewelry to a man who sat in a partially enclosed cubicle in the back of the store. They consulted in whispers and the older man stared across the store at her before carefully examining the jewels one by one. At length he shrugged and nodded. The first man returned to Caprice. ''Is there any particular reason you wish to return these?''

''The pearls are too long and the emeralds are the wrong shade,'' she said.

''This is very unusual, Mrs. Banning. We have often done business with your family, but this is the first time any of you have been displeased. I hope it won't affect our dealings in the future.'' He seemed genuinely concerned.

"It won't," Caprice reassured him. "I'm not displeased with the workmanship, it's just that I had something else in mind."

With relief he said, "Perhaps an exchange then. We have a lovely ruby necklace I could show you."

"No thank you. Rubies aren't right for my coloring. I'll come in and look around when I have more time."

After explaining that she wanted the refund deposited to her checking account, she headed to a bank where she wouldn't be recognized as Caprice Banning to open a joint account in the names of Katherine Farnell and Caprice Dolan.

Caprice's hand trembled as she signed her name on the signature card at the new accounts desk. She felt terribly guilty and avoided looking anyone in the eye. She handed the clerk twenty-five dollars in cash to open the account and slipped the duplicate signature card that she had to get signed by Katie into her purse. Within the week, she would go to her bank and withdraw the refunded money from her account and deposit the cashier's check for fifty thousand in the joint account she had just set up. When the bank clerk tapped her arm to get her attention so she could tell her that her printed checks would be sent within the next ten days, Caprice almost jumped out of her skin. Nervously taking the slim folder of temporary checks and deposit slips, Caprice quickly left the bank.

Her knees were weak, and she had an unpleasant fluttering sensation in her stomach. She got into her car and started it, but for several minutes she sat there, staring straight ahead. Why did she feel so terribly guilty? Luke had given her those things as gifts. If she chose to return them, that was her prerogative. But to take the money seemed terribly wrong.

Out of nervous habit, Caprice chewed on her lower lip as she attempted to rationalize her actions. Why should it matter whether she kept the gifts or the money? she mused. Luke had given them to her to make her happy, and how could she be happy with those things knowing that Heather needed money for an operation to save her life? It only made sense to take the cash.

Because of Houston's warm climate, she had no reason to wear the furs for at least another month and probably longer. However, the absence of the diamonds and emeralds would be harder to explain. She decided to tell Luke that she wasn't wearing them because she was saving them for a very special occasion. And the pearls?

She drove to a less expensive department store and bought a rope of high-quality imitation pearls. They were so close in size and color that she doubted anyone would ever suspect they weren't the expensive originals.

She looped the pearls around her neck and decided to tell Luke she was so fond of them that she chose to wear them instead of the emeralds. It was risky, but she had no other ideas.

Caprice's mind was so preoccupied, she again didn't notice the tan car that followed half a block behind her. The car tailed her all the way to the Heights.

Heather was sitting on the porch when Caprice pulled up and parked at the curb. Her eyes lit up when she saw her aunt, and she came down the front walk to meet her.

"Is your Mom home?" Caprice asked, noticing the blue circles beneath the girl's eyes. Heather was thinner, too, and she lacked her usual buoyant spirit.

"She's inside. Guess what, Aunt Cappy? Dad's home!"

Caprice looked sharply at the small house. "He is?"

"He came home last night. Isn't that great?"

"It sure is, honey." She turned back to her niece. "Shouldn't you be inside resting? Dr. Granger said you should have a nap every afternoon."

"I know, but Dad said I could come outside for a while."

"I see." Caprice squared her shoulders and headed for the front door. It was just like Jed Farnell to countermand the doctor's orders.

Without knocking, Caprice entered the house, and for a moment she could see very little as her eyes adjusted from the bright sunlight outside to the dimly lit interior. Katie and her husband were sitting on the couch, and appeared to have been kissing when Caprice walked in.

"Have you forgotten how to knock?" the man said as he stood up.

"Hello, Jed. I saw no reason to knock since I've lived here for quite a while now. Or did." She studied him cautiously. He was still handsome in a slick sort of a way. Drinking and hard living had etched lines at the corners of his eyes and loosened the skin under his chin, but Jed still had his looks.

Katie, who had a smile plastered across her face, was glowing as if she were a girl in the first blush of love. "Jed came home last night. Isn't it wonderful?"

"Yes." Caprice couldn't bring herself to say more. Especially not when Jed was giving her the smug grin that meant he always got his way.

"Heather and I were watching TV last night when he just walked in!"

"Where have you been, Jed?" Caprice challenged.

"Here and there."

"I was just telling Jed that you got married," Katie added.

"But she didn't say who to." He strolled closer to Caprice, his black eyes studying her from head to toe. "Looks like you did okay for yourself. Who's the lucky fellow?"

Caprice shot her sister a warning glare. "You don't know him." To Katie she said, "Why is Heather outside? You know she needs her rest now that school has started again."

"She's a kid," Jed said offhandedly. "She needs to be outside in the sunshine."

"Didn't you tell him how sick Heather is?" Caprice demanded of her sister.

"Well, Jed's her father, and—"

"Hell, those doctors don't know nothing," Jed interrupted. "My sister was pale and skinny as a kid. Heather just takes after her."

"It's a lot more than that," Caprice said stiffly. "We've taken her to a specialist, and he said Heather is very sick. She has to have a liver transplant or she will die.''

''Nah, I don't believe it. Those doctors will say anything to get your money. She just needs to get away from your mollycoddling. You always have spoiled her rotten.''

As if she had heard her name, Heather poked her head in the door. ''What's for supper, Mom?''

''Pork chops,'' Katie said.

''Good. Are you staying to eat with us, Aunt Cappy?''

''No, I have to go home before then.''

Jed said, ''Maybe you could go visit Aunt Cappy for a few days, Heather. Give me and your mama a chance to get reacquainted.''

Katie frowned at her husband, but before she could speak, Heather said, ''I can't do that. We're supposed to be a secret.''

''A what? A secret?'' Jed's black brows drew together. ''A secret from who?''

''Heather, go out and play,'' Katie ordered in a tone that meant Heather had better obey promptly. The girl turned and closed the door behind her.

Jed stuffed his fingers into his jeans pockets and looked from one woman to the other. ''What the hell is she talking about?''

''How should I know?'' Katie said testily. ''You know what an imagination she has.''

He went to Caprice, who met his gaze steadily. ''Maybe Miss High-and-Mighty here ain't married at all. How about it, Caprice? Did you find yourself a sugar daddy?''

Caprice wanted to slap the smirk from his face, but managed to restrain herself. "You know me better than that, Jed."

"Yeah, I guess I do at that." He stepped back, but he continued to study her. "You know, there's something funny about all this. You always have put on airs around me, but now you're dressed nice and you even talk different."

"It's nothing, Jed," Katie said with an attempt at a laugh. "You know how well Caprice sews. She can make clothes that look like they came from Neiman's."

He nodded as he narrowed his eyes. "Maybe so, but she can't make jewelry as far as I know."

"These are fakes," Caprice said as she removed the paste pearls. "Here. Do you want them?"

He paused as he tried to determine whether she was bluffing. "What about that ring? It looks real to me."

"It really does, doesn't it?" Caprice said lightly. "They can do wonders with costume jewelry these days."

Jed rubbed his jaw as Caprice put the pearls back around her neck. "Katie, go get me another beer."

Katie did Jed's bidding, and Caprice felt very awkward being alone with him. To fill the silence, she said, "Jed, Heather really is sick. Maybe if you went to Mr. Homer over at the construction company, he might take you back on as foreman."

"Nah, he fired me."

"Well, what are your plans? Katie needs your income. There are the doctor bills and prescriptions, and soon Heather will need an operation. Katie can't support you and pay for all that as well."

"I told you Heather ain't sick. She's just like my kid sister used to be. Carrie grew out of it, and so will Heather."

"No, Jed, she won't. Without that operation she won't live that long." She felt as if the slender bank book she had brought for Katie must be visible in her purse. It had been a mistake to put it in Katie's name because, as her husband, Jed might be able to get access to it. Fifty thousand dollars would send Jed Farnell on quite a spree, and Katie would be powerless to stop him. She was putty in Jed's hands and Caprice knew Jed wouldn't hesitate to use force to get the money. No, she couldn't let Katie know about the bank account. Not yet.

He took the beer as Katie came back into the room. "Well, aren't you even going to sit down?" he asked Caprice.

"No. No, I have to be going."

"Come on, take Heather with you for a couple of days," Jed wheedled. "Katie and I have some catching up to do."

Caprice looked at him with distaste. "I'm afraid that's quite impossible."

"Hear how she talks?" he said to Katie. "She sounds like something out of a picture."

"Speaking correctly isn't a personality flaw, Jed." Caprice drew herself up proudly.

"You don't care much for me, do you?"

"I don't care for you at all."

"Jed, Cappy, please don't start fussing," Katie said anxiously as she stepped between them. "Jed just came home. Let's all try to forget and forgive. Can't you do that, Caprice?"

"I have nothing to forgive him for. He didn't desert *me*."

Katie hurried to her sister. "Don't start up with him. He might leave again, and then where would we be?" Her worried eyes searched Caprice's face pleadingly.

Caprice relented. "Where indeed? If this is how you want it, Katie, it's up to you. It's your life. But you have to convince him that Heather really is seriously ill."

"I will, I will. After he's had a chance to watch her a few days, he'll understand. He's her daddy, after all. He wants the best for her."

Caprice looked past her sister to Jed, who had a brooding expression. "Of course. Did you have the phone reconnected?" When Katie nodded, Caprice said, "I'll call you tomorrow to see how she is."

"Okay. Jed will be out looking for work, but I'll be in at five o'clock."

Caprice nodded. She suspected Jed would look no farther than the nearest bar.

She told Heather goodbye on the porch and drove away through the narrow streets toward the freeway. Behind her the tan car followed faithfully.

Luke scowled at Ralph and leaned menacingly across the desk. "You've done what?"

"I did it for your own good. After all, you knew very little about her, and..."

"You had her followed?" Luke was so angry he trembled with the effort to control himself.

"As it turned out, that was a prudent move." Using the tips of his manicured fingers, Ralph pushed a manilla folder toward Luke. "There are some very curious things going on here. For instance, she has withdrawn her allowance and an additional fifty thousand dollars, as well."

"From her own account? Where did the money come from?"

"I have no idea. Also, she has been seen going to a house in the Heights on—" he consulted his notes "—Bixby Street."

"Bixby? I never heard of it."

"Apparently she knows it quite well. She's been there several times."

"In the Heights? Well, she must have a friend there."

"This isn't the sort of house where one would expect to find a Banning. From all accounts it's in pretty bad shape."

"Who lives there?"

"It's a rented house. Morris Ainsley contacted the owner, but he refused to say who is renting it. He says it's none of our business. The audacity of some people."

"Well, I'm sure it isn't any of our business!"

"However, Ainsley took down the license plate number from an old Ford sedan parked at the house. It's registered to a Jed Farnell."

Luke's face darkened. "What exactly are you trying to tell me, Ralph?"

"Only that something very odd is going on. First she withdraws all that money, then there are the visits to this house."

"Visits? How many?"

"She's been there four times since you two returned from the cruise."

Luke straightened up and paced to the window. "I'm sure there's a reasonable explanation for all of this."

"The withdrawal of fifty thousand dollars puts her in direct violation of her marriage contract."

"But it wasn't my fifty thousand. Where did it come from?"

"We haven't verified that as yet. Ainsley is working on that. The bank is due for an audit soon, and he says one of the federal auditors owes him a big favor. It looks very suspicious, though. The contract she signed clearly states that her monthly withdrawals are not to exceed five thousand a month without your approval."

"Are you suggesting I should fire her?" Luke asked acidly.

"Unfortunately, that's not possible. There's something else. This afternoon the jeweler from Doneby's called and asked why you were dissatisfied with the necklace, bracelet, and pearls."

"What?"

"It seems Mrs. Banning returned them."

"She did what?"

"Naturally they didn't give her cash for them, but it's odd she would take them back, isn't it?" Ralph looked at Luke through his thick lenses. "So I took the liberty of checking with Neiman's about the furs."

"You have taken a great many liberties, Ralph."

"She returned the furs as well."

"That doesn't make any sense!"

"I know."

Several seconds ticked by before Luke said, "I'll look into this. In the meantime, call off Ainsley and don't do anything like this again. You're a good man, Ralph, and I would hate to lose you, but I can't allow this to happen again."

"I understand. Luke," he said as his employer strode toward the door. "I wish I had been wrong."

Luke paused, then continued on his way. There had to be some explanation for all of this. True, Caprice had been reluctant to buy so much, but he had assumed she was protesting in order not to seem greedy. Evidently she really hadn't wanted the furs and jewels. What woman wouldn't want fur and jewels?

He went to the living room and sank into an armchair. Beyond the window he could see Caprice sitting by the pool, reading a novel as if she had done nothing at all wrong. He picked up the telephone receiver and got the number for Wellesley College.

"Hello, registrar's office? I'd like to check on a former student of yours. Caprice Dolan. She would have been there about three years ago...No? Would you check five years ago?...I see. Thank you."

Slowly Luke hung up the phone. Caprice Dolan had never attended Wellesley College. He watched her as he tried to figure out why she would have lied about it. Perhaps she was simply embarrassed at not having a college degree, but why didn't she have one? Everyone he knew had at least one degree.

Perhaps she had simply lied about her age. No, he decided, she couldn't have graduated over five years earlier. She looked too young. If anything, he had wondered if she were as old as she said, not the other way around.

Above all, who was this Jed Farnell? Memories of Paulette and her flagrant affairs assailed him. Surely Caprice wasn't like that! Even if she were, why would she pick a man who lived in the Heights? Where would she even meet such a man?

He strolled out to the pool, and Caprice jumped when his shadow fell over her. "Did I startle you? I'm sorry," he said.

"It's all right. I didn't hear you come out."

"I was just thinking." He bent over her and braced his palms on the arms of her chair. "I read a scene once in a book that I would like to try." His tone was seductive and not at all suggestive of his suspicion.

"Oh?" she asked with a smile. "Tell me about it."

He leaned forward to kiss her as he said, "There was a woman in the book who wanted to attract her lover's attention." He left a string of kisses over her cheek and down her neck as he spoke. "So she put on a full-length mink and nothing else. Then she let him discover she had nothing on at all under the coat. Does that sound interesting?"

"Fascinating." She seemed a bit uneasy, but she didn't take the opportunity to tell him about returning the furs.

"Why don't you get your fur coat and let's try it out."

She blinked, then said, "I have a better idea. Let's cut out the middleman and not waste any time." She smiled mischievously. "Or better yet, I read a scene once where the seductress wore only whipped cream and cherries. I'll get some from the kitchen and meet you in the bedroom before you can draw the drapes." She kissed him lightly and scampered toward the back door.

Luke didn't try to stop her. He wasn't sure what to think. Was she avoiding telling him about the coat or did she really have whipped cream in mind?

He went to their room and, with a twinge of guilt, opened her closet door. A quick survey turned up no fur coats.

"Luke? What are you looking for?" Caprice stood in the doorway, a can of whipped cream in one hand and a bottle of maraschino cherries in the other.

"Your fur coats. They aren't in here."

"I put them in storage," she said smoothly. "I won't need them for a while." She advanced with a tempting smile. "I found the goodies. I don't think Mrs. Thompson or Juanita saw me take them. I feel positively decadent."

Luke was puzzled. As he went to her, he saw the rope of pearls curled in the box where she kept them. He lifted them, each globe shimmering and fragile. Ralph had said she had returned the pearls along with the other gifts. Yet here they were. None of this made any sense. He had thought at first that the fifty thousand might have come from a refund on the furs and jewelry, but Ralph had said they didn't give her a cash refund. And now the pearls were still here and she said the furs were in storage. Perhaps the stores had been wrong. The fifty thousand could have been her own money that she had deposited to her account from another bank, then later withdrew. He wouldn't even allow himself to think about the Farnell man from Bixby Street.

"Luke? Is something wrong?"

Pushing all the discomforting thoughts from his mind, he smiled and took her into his arms. "Yes, you're wearing too many clothes." He gave himself up to her loving and let the world and all his concerns drift away.

Chapter Twelve

Jed sat up in bed and lazily scratched his stomach as he squinted at the clock. Katie had left to take Heather to school an hour before and wouldn't be home from work until after five. He yawned as he rolled out of bed and stretched. He had the day to himself.

He went into the kitchen and poured a cup of coffee from the pot Katie had brewed. She had washed the dishes before she left for work, but Jed didn't care about such things. Katie's compulsive neatness got on his nerves. He made himself some toast and ate it as he drank the black coffee. He had been home only a week, and he was bored already.

Katie had started by hinting that he should get a job, but lately her barbs had been more than just hints. Jed hated pushy women, and he was tempted to pack up and leave again while the house was quiet.

He thought of the little brunette he had left in the Smokys. Mary Jane, that was her name. She might welcome him back. She had put up a big fuss when he left, and it hadn't been so long that she was likely to have found a replacement for him, as yet. But the Smokys were a long way from Houston, and his car had been acting up.

Then there was Sally. They had parted with angry words just before he came back to town, but even Sally would have calmed down by now. No, he thought, Sally had been getting as possessive as Katie. If he had to have someone acting like a wife, he might as well have the one he married. At least Katie knew her place. Besides, Sally lived in Louisiana, and Jed was avoiding that state for a while.

He ground out his cigarette in the saucer and set his dirty coffee cup on the table before stepping out back for a breath of fresh air. The grass needed mowing, what there was of it, and the paint was peeling badly off of the house. The last time he had painted, he had done only the part that showed from the street. In back, the paint had flaked down to the bare wood, which looked gray and soft.

Jed ambled back inside, wondering how he was going to spend the day. He didn't have any money to go to a bar, and Katie wouldn't get paid for another week. He gave some thought to going to the bus station to try to con some lonely old woman into a bus ticket to the Smoky Mountains, but he gave up the idea. Jed hated to admit it, but he didn't think his looks were as spectacular as they once had been, and he was mortally afraid of rejection.

With nothing else to do, he went back to the bedroom he shared with Katie and sat on the side of the rumpled bed. Methodically he went through the drawers where Katie kept the odds and ends of her life. He wasn't looking for anything in particular, but sometimes the drawers yielded enough loose change to buy a beer.

When he found the fold of heavy paper, he almost tossed it aside, but its luxurious thickness caught his attention. It was pale blue, a flourishing "B" was monogrammed on the top. Jed opened the note and read simply a phone number and address. No name.

With a frown, Jed turned the paper over, then reopened it. What was this? No one he knew used paper like this. Was Katie fooling around on him? He took the paper to the phone and dialed the number. After two rings the phone was answered.

"Banning residence," a deep voice said.

Jed hung up. Banning? He didn't know anyone by that name. As he puzzled over what this could mean, an idea began to take shape. The man's voice had sounded like a servant's to Jed. Surely if the man who had answered the phone had been the owner, he would have just said "hello" like anybody else.

He remembered how Caprice had looked on her visit the day after he came back. She was wearing fine clothes that didn't look homemade to him. Then there was that ring that she had said was fake but was as shiny as the real thing, and a string of pearls long enough to rope a calf!

Once again he dialed the number. The deep voice answered without a trace of annoyance at being summoned again. This time Jed said, "Is Caprice there?"

"One moment please."

Caprice was drawing sketches for an evening gown as Luke read the paper. "I have had an idea," she said as her pencil added a few finishing touches. "There's nothing for me to do all day, so I've decided to design a line of clothes. What do you think?" She handed him the sketch and anxiously watched his face.

"This is really good!" he said, obviously surprised. "I didn't know you could draw like this."

"Do you like the dress?"

"Yes, I like it a lot."

"I've always wanted to design clothes. What do you really think? Can I do it? Would I be good enough?"

"I don't know anything about designing clothes, but I like this sketch. If you want to do it, I think you should give it a try."

Caprice looked up as Lawford came into the room. The butler still intimidated her.

"Telephone, Mrs. Banning." He plugged the phone into a nearby jack and handed it to her.

"Hello?"

"So your married name is Banning, is it?" Jed said in a taunting voice.

Caprice nearly dropped the phone when she recognized the voice on the other end.

"How did you . . . . Is it Heather? Nothing has happened, has it?" She could feel Luke's gaze upon her back, and she gripped the receiver tightly.

"Nah, she's fine. I found this phone number and put two and two together. You know what I think, Caprice? I think you did find yourself a sugar daddy after all."

Caprice hung up so hard the phone jingled.

"Honey? Is something wrong?" Luke leaned forward with concern.

"No! No, nothing is wrong." She tried to still her trembling hands. What if Jed showed up on her doorstep! He would ruin everything! She tried desperately to remember if she also gave Katie her address or just the phone number.

"Something is wrong. You're shaking."

"It was an...an obscene call," she stammered out. "He seemed to know me, and it frightened me."

"I wonder how anyone could get this number? He must have been dialing at random."

"Yes. Yes, that must have been it." Even as she spoke, the phone rang again.

"Let me answer it," Luke said as he reached for it.

Caprice grabbed it up and said, "Hello!"

"You hung up on me," Jed said. "That was a mistake, Caprice. It makes me think you're hiding something."

"Don't you dare call back here again!" Once more she slammed down the phone.

"Was it the same caller?" Luke asked.

She could only nod. Hesitantly she lifted the phone and was relieved to hear a dial tone. She laid the receiver on the table.

"Honey, what could he say that would upset you so much? Should we call the police?"

"No!"

"If he threatened you . . ."

"No, no. It was nothing like that. It . . . it just frightened me."

"I'll call the telephone company if it continues."

"Yes. Yes, that might be a good idea. If it continues." She stood up and said, "Will you excuse me for a minute?"

Luke looked at her curiously, but said, "Of course. Caprice, are you sure you're okay?"

"I'm fine." She turned and almost ran from the room.

She knew the phone in Ralph's office was on another line and that he was out on business at the moment. Although she knew she was taking a chance, she went into his office and shut the door. Quickly she dialed the number of the Sunny Day Caterers and asked for Katie. Keeping her voice low so no one would hear her, Caprice said, "Jed found my number and called here!"

"He did? When?"

"Just now!"

"He told me he was going to be job-hunting all day."

"Katie, don't you understand? He could ruin everything. If he had asked an odd question when Lawford answered the phone, or if he had spoken to Luke and not to me, he could have created a real problem."

"What can I do about it? I'm at work now. Besides, I can't keep Jed from using the phone in his own house."

"You can tell him not to call me!"

"Look, Caprice, I have to get off the phone. You know how Mr. Haynes is about personal calls at work. We'll have to talk later."

"Katie, you do something! Jed might listen to you!"

"I have to go. Unlike you, I work for a living, and I can't afford to make my boss mad at me."

Caprice slowly hung up. She was stung as well as frightened by Katie's parting barb. She knew all too well that Katie had no control over Jed. For a moment she sat there in Ralph's antiseptically clean office trying to think of what she could do to protect herself. Realizing she couldn't possibly explain her presence in this office if someone should walk in, Caprice jumped up and hurried back into the hall. Her instincts had proved correct, for as she entered the main wing of the house, she saw Ralph returning from his business errand. She nodded to him coolly and kept going. She had far more than Ralph Slayton to worry about.

Caprice was nervous all morning. At noon she scarcely tasted the Caesar salad, which was one of her favorites. All her efforts went toward convincing Luke that she was no longer upset over the phone calls she had received that morning.

"I have to go downtown," Luke said when Juanita had cleared away the meal. "Are you all right here? You can come with me if you like and shop while I have my meetings."

"No, thanks." She made herself smile as if nothing at all were wrong. She didn't dare leave the house and risk having Jed call while she was gone. "I want to draw up some more designs and put together a portfolio."

"I'm glad you're doing that," Luke said. "I had been concerned that you would get bored. Why don't you call Christine and meet her at the country club for tennis or go shopping? She's had time to cool off, and you two might become friends."

"Maybe I will," Caprice hedged. She had no intention of doing any such thing. Luke accepted her because he loved her, and he obviously excused her occasional slips as eccentricities, but Christine might see right through her.

She took out her sketch pad and drew a few preliminary designs as Luke dressed in a suit and tie in preparation for his business meetings. Although her mind kept wandering, her skillful fingers produced one flowing creation after another. Caprice polished the best of these into finished sketches.

Luke came in and bent to kiss her. His gray eyes looked worried, and Caprice was touched at his protectiveness. Without a word she smiled up at him and stroked his smoothly shaven cheek. He returned her smile before bending lower to kiss her.

Despite her pretence at casualness, Caprice felt very much alone and very vulnerable when he was gone. True, Lawford and Juanita were somewhere in the house, and Mrs. Thompson was as near as the kitchen, but she felt insecure. What if Jed called again? As a safeguard, she removed the phone from its cradle and muffled the dial tone by shoving it under a pillow.

Laying the sketch pad aside, Caprice stood up and paced the length of the room. She couldn't concentrate for worrying. Her pacing carried her to the bookshelf where she paused. Luke had given her the combination to his wall safe and had shown her how to deactivate the alarm and open it, but she had never tried it on her own. She removed the books that covered the safe, turned off the alarm, and whirled the dial in the manner he had shown her. When she had turned it to the last number and pulled down on the handle, it clicked softly, then opened. Inside were numerous papers, but the things that caught her attention were the large stacks of bills.

Caprice had no idea how much money was there, but she knew it was far more than she had ever seen. With great curiosity, she removed one of the bundles of one-hundred-dollar bills and began to leaf through the stack when a movement at the corner of her eye startled her. She jerked around to find Ralph watching her. "You frightened me!" she gasped as she tried to catch her breath.

"Oh? I didn't mean to." He watched her intently as if he thought it quite odd to find her taking money from the safe. "I deposited your monthly allowance in the bank this morning."

"I wasn't..." She stopped herself before she began making excuses like a guilty child. "Thank you," she amended. As if she had seen what she wanted to see, Caprice replaced the money in the vault, relocked it, and put the books back in place. Trying to look as nonchalant as she could, she reactivated the alarm system.

Ralph was still watching her.

"Yes?" she said almost angrily.

"I was wondering if Luke has left yet for his meetings."

"Yes, he has." She frowned at Ralph before saying, "Why don't you like me? I mean only to make Luke happy."

"Not like you? I have no idea what you mean. It's not up to me to care about you one way or another."

"Don't hand me that. You know what I mean."

"I saw Luke hurt badly by his first wife. He's the closest friend I've ever had, and I don't want to see him hurt again."

"He loves me and I love him."

"I find it amazing that you clearly feel the need to defend yourself to me—if you've nothing to hide."

Caprice bit back her words. He was right. She mustn't protest too much. "And I find it amazing that you assume I am defending myself."

Ralph gave her the smallest of smiles. "Touché." He waved the papers he held in his hand. "Luke forgot these. If he comes back, they're right here." He laid them on an end table and left as quietly as he had come.

Caprice felt weak in the knees. Ralph suspected her! She was positive of that. But how and why? She couldn't think of any slip she had made in his presence. As nervous as he made her, she was always doubly careful when he was around.

Caprice went to the front window and looked out on the sun-dappled lawn. Even after this short a time, she felt she belonged here. The duplicity that had brought her here seemed to be the act of another woman. She loved Luke with all her heart and really did want only his happiness. The scheme she and Katie had worked out was more a fantasy than the life she was living.

As she stood there looking out, an all too familiar battered Ford pulled into her drive, and her first thought was that it couldn't really be happening. Even when the car stopped and Jed got out, she felt this was a hallucination, a nightmare. Then he was on the front walk, and she knew it was all too real.

She ran to the front door and stepped out, closing it behind her. "What are you doing here?" she whispered.

He stopped abruptly as if he hadn't been sure until now that the address was correct. "So this is your new house. Well, now. No wonder Heather said we have to be kept secret. How in the hell did you marry a Banning?" He stepped closer.

Caprice pressed her back against the door. "Get out of here, Jed! You don't want to force me to have you thrown off the property." She thought of Lawford's white-gloved hands and Ralph's slight build. She wasn't sure either of them were a match for Jed's brawl-roughened muscles.

"You won't do that. Not and let it be known that I'm married to your sister. You know what I think? I think this Banning doesn't have any idea where you come from or who you really are. Am I right?"

"No! Now get out of my yard!"

He chuckled menacingly. "Don't threaten me, Caprice."

"Look, Jed, this is very important. It's the only way we can get the money we need for Heather's operation."

"Bull," he said with a grin. "There ain't no way I'm going to believe that."

"Believe whatever you please, but it's true. Now get out of here before someone sees you."

Jed rested his fingertips in his jeans pockets and looked speculatively at the house and grounds. "Nice place you have here. I bet it cost a fortune."

"Luke is here," she bluffed, "and if you don't leave..."

"Luke? Luke Banning?" Jed whistled appreciatively. "You picked yourself a plum, Cappy girl. No wonder you're so fancy these days." He looked at her with sexual appraisal. "Now I really do wonder how you managed to get him to marry you. Maybe you've got talents I never dreamed of."

She glared at her brother-in-law in disgust. "I told you, my husband is home. Don't make me call him!"

"Go ahead. Call him out here. It's time the families met." Again he looked around. "Yeah, this is some setup."

Caprice felt sick when she realized Jed had no intention of leaving. At any moment, Lawford, or worse still, Ralph, might look out and see him.

"Yeah, I'll bet Banning has no idea at all he married a seamstress who only hitched up with him for his money."

"It's not like that. At least not now. I love him."

Jed grinned broadly. "You've already said you married him to get money for Heather. Maybe you could get money for me, too."

"What!"

"Just call it blackmail," he said with a laugh. "That's what it is."

"Blackmail!"

"I think I could see my way clear to forget where I found you for, oh, maybe three hundred dollars. What do you say?"

"You've got to be kidding!"

"Of course that's just the first installment. By the end of the month I want a thousand."

"A thousand dollars! I can't do that!"

"Yes, you can. Otherwise I'm going to go inside and have a long talk with your new husband."

Caprice considered bluffing him, but she had too much to lose. A few words from Jed and she not only wouldn't have Luke, she couldn't save Heather. "Wait here," she said angrily.

She left him in the front yard and hurried back to the wall safe. If she gave him three hundred from it, she could write a check from her account and replace it before it was missed—she hoped.

When she returned, Jed was sitting on the doorstep as if he owned the place. At her approach he got to his feet and held out his hand. Methodically he counted the bills. "You keep cash like this laying around? Got any more?"

"No! Now get out of here!"

He grinned again. "I don't believe you, but I can wait two weeks for the rest." He shoved the money in his pocket and sauntered back to the car. "Just bring the rest to the house and save me a trip."

Caprice felt as if she had been turned to stone. He got in the car and drove away, but just as he left the driveway, Luke pulled in. Caprice wondered if she were going to faint on the spot, but she had never fainted in her life and didn't then.

Luke parked exactly where Jed had and came to her. "Who was that?"

"Who?" Here eyes were round with fright and her palms were clammy.

"That man who just drove away from here. I nearly ran into him as I was turning in."

"Oh. Him. He was asking about a job. As gardener."

"Odd. We haven't advertised for a gardener, and why would one come to the front door?"

"I have no idea."

"Next time let Lawford handle it. You shouldn't have to bother with things like that." He passed her and went into the house. "I forgot my papers for the meeting."

"They're right there on the end table." She stood with tightly clasped hands as he picked up the typed sheets.

"Thanks, honey. I'll be home in a couple of hours." He dropped a kiss on her lips and refrained from frowning as he went back to his car. He had been close enough to get a good look at the man backing out of his driveway, and the man didn't look like any gardener Luke had ever seen. True the old car and the man's appearance had been pretty low, but his face was handsome in a cheap sort of way. Paulette's escapades came immediately to mind, even though Paulette would never have looked at anyone who didn't drive a Rolls.

Something about that car tugged at his memory. Hadn't Ralph said something about a Ford in front of the house Caprice supposedly visited in the Heights? Jealousy stung him, and a muscle tightened in his jaw. Who was this man? He had heard of women who liked affairs with men below their social station. But not Caprice! He simply couldn't believe she would be unfaithful, and especially not with a man who looked like a cut-rate gigolo!

As soon as Luke drove away, Caprice went to the bedroom and shut the door, then called Katie. ''I don't care if you are at work, Jed was here!''

''That's impossible. How would he know where you are?''

''I don't know. I must have jotted down my address as well as my phone number for you. Katie, he's blackmailing me!'' There was a long silence. ''Katie, did you hear me?''

''Caprice, I can't believe you would say such a thing about Jed.''

''It's true! I just gave him three hundred dollars, and he says he needs a thousand by the end of the month.''

''What? I don't believe you. Jed is my husband. He wouldn't do such a thing.'' There was a muffled exchange of words, and Katie said in a low voice, ''I have to get off the phone.''

"What you have to do is get Jed off my back! You have to make him stop blackmailing me!"

"We'll talk about it later."

"We have to talk about it now!"

"If I don't hang up, I'll get fired!" Katie's voice rose in anger.

"It'll be easier for you to find another job than for me to find another Luke Banning. Even if you don't care about my happiness, think about your daughter. Don't you see that Jed is about to ruin everything? Tell him again about Heather. Make him understand."

"I've tried. I even had Dr. Granger call him, but Jed only believes what he wants to. He doesn't think she's sick at all."

"Well, at least stop him from blackmailing me! Katie, I can't pay it *and* take care of Heather!"

"You needn't take that attitude with me," Katie said in a brittle voice. "I don't believe for a minute Jed has been over there! I think you're just saying that because you don't want to help me with Heather anymore! I should have known you'd turn on me once you became one of them!"

"Katie!" Caprice gasped.

"Furthermore, my job is important to me. Maybe *you* don't need to work, but *I* do." Katie slammed down the receiver.

Caprice stared at the dead phone for a full minute before she hung up. Tears of bewilderment stung her eyes. What had happened to her life? Uncontrollable trembling began deep within her and spread right to her fingertips.

She lay on the bed and curled into a tight knot. After talking to Katie she knew she could never go back to being Caprice Dolan. And if Jed persisted, she might not be Caprice Banning either. The thought of losing Luke sent a bone-deep pain through her.

She would pay for Heather's operation somehow. Katie's abandonment didn't change Caprice's love for her niece. And once the operation was behind her, and Heather was healthy, Caprice would spend the rest of her life trying to be the best wife Luke could ever have—if her marriage lasted that long.

Caprice gave up and let herself cry until all her tears were gone.

Chapter Thirteen

As Caprice drove the new white Mercedes Luke had bought her off the freeway and onto the exit into the Heights, she wished she could somehow return it as she had the furs and jewels. She loved the car and it handled as smoothly as if its wheels didn't touch the road, but she could see only the money it represented. Money that Heather couldn't have.

In her leather purse was a thousand dollars in cash. She had the impression that blackmail was always paid in cash—presumably so the victim couldn't change her mind and stop payment on a check and so that the blackmailer's name wasn't written down anywhere. Caprice had withdrawn the cash he had demanded, even though it galled her.

She was relieved to see Katie's station wagon parked in front of Jed's Ford in the driveway. She hadn't wanted to find herself alone with him. When he had called the day before to remind her to bring the money, some of his insinuations had been a bit too suggestive for comfort.

This time she knocked on the door and waited for Katie to open it before she went in. The strain between the sisters was almost visible as Caprice stiffly asked, "Is Jed here?"

"He's in the kitchen," Katie answered as she shut the door behind Caprice and preceded her through the house as if Caprice were a stranger.

Jed was sitting at the table, his shirt off, smoking a cigarette and drinking a cup of black coffee. Hearing someone enter, he glanced up, Then, when he saw who it was, he took one final drag off his cigarette and snuffed it out in an ashtray before speaking. "Hello, Caprice. I was wondering what was keeping you."

Caprice withdrew an envelope from her bag and silently thrust it at Jed. The man greedily tore it open and began counting the bills. Caprice's eyes met Katie's as she said, "Now do you believe me, Katie?"

Her sister looked away as she said, "It doesn't prove anything. You gave me four thousand last month."

Jed's eyes widened as Caprice gasped. "Katie!" she snapped.

"That's real generous of you," Jed said thoughtfully. "This sure will help us out."

"Don't play innocent with me, Jed. I'm not giving you this money because I want to. Katie, if you use my money to live better and buy things for yourself, how

will you ever save enough for Heather's operation?''
She pointed accusingly at a new refrigerator that stuck
out like a sore thumb in the kitchen. ''You bought that
with the money I gave you, didn't you!'' It occurred
to her that not telling Katie yet about the fifty thousand dollars she had deposited to the new joint account had been a good decision.

''My old one quit running. I had to have a refrigerator,'' Katie defended herself hotly.

''You're smarter than that!'' Caprice exploded.
''You should have bought a secondhand one or a
cheaper model, not the top of the line.''

''Do *you* have a secondhand one? Ever since you
married Luke Banning you've become just like them.
You look down your nose at us and begrudge us
everything we get that's new.''

''Katie, have you changed this much or have I? You
aren't like the sister I knew. You're a stranger to me.''

''Well, I could say the same about you. When you
lived here, you would have been tickled to death to get
a new refrigerator.''

''What about Heather's operation?''

Katie shrugged. ''You've got Luke Banning's millions. You can surely get a measly two hundred thousand for your own niece.''

Caprice's eyes were as green and as hard as the emerald in her wedding ring as she stared at Katie in ut-
ter disbelief. Katie glared back for a moment, then
defiantly crossed her arms and turned away. ''I don't
know you anymore,'' Caprice said quietly. ''I don't
know if we have changed or if this mess we're in has
just brought out facets of our personalities that we've

never seen before. At any rate, I'm so sorry it's happened, because I know we can never be what we once were to each other. I'll get the money for Heather, although it's far more difficult than you seem to think. After that, I think it would be best if we not see as much of each other."

"That's fine with me," Katie replied tersely, her back rigid as if she were fighting to hold back tears.

Caprice turned and walked hurriedly through the house before she burst into tears on the spot. When she reached the front door she was startled to find Jed beside her.

"Next month make it two thousand," he said in a low voice.

She met his eyes with extreme contempt, but managed not to answer. With relief, she escaped out the door.

When she arrived home, she saw Christine's Lincoln parked out front. Her first impulse was to keep driving, but she knew she couldn't avoid her sister-in-law forever, so she pulled into the covered parking space at the side of the house. That Christine might still be angry over Luke's choice of wife wasn't as bothersome to Caprice as her fear that the woman would be able to see through the ruse and expose her for what she was: a fraud.

She let herself in through a door at the rear of the house, and as she made her way to the sunroom, she tried to convince herself that her fear was without basis. As she had expected, Luke and Christine were there, engaged in conversation.

When Caprice entered, Christine stopped talking, and for a strained moment no one said a word. Then Luke went to Caprice and put his arm about her. "Honey, this is Christine. Christine, this is Caprice. Christine was just telling me of an idea for fund-raising that she and Philippa Hadley had thought up."

"Fund-raising?" Caprice asked.

"Yes, for needy children," Christine explained. "The Pin Oak Charity Horse Show has been such a success, we thought a charity polo match would go over well."

"What needy children did you have in mind?"

"I got the idea when I saw one of those donation cans at a cash register. This particular case was a boy needing a kidney transplant. Philippa and I thought it would be a marvelous idea to sponsor a yearly polo match and use the proceeds for poor children in need of medical treatment."

Caprice could hardly believe what she was hearing. She eased herself onto the edge of the sofa.

"Don't you think it's a good idea?" Luke prompted.

"I think it's wonderful!" Caprice said. "How will these children be chosen?"

"Philippa has called surgeons from each of the hospitals in the medical center and asked them to submit a list of patients who are in financial straits. From the combined list we will choose the most needy and pay for their operations."

"Which doctors did she contact?" Caprice breathed a sigh of relief when Dr. Eugene Granger's name was mentioned. Surely Heather's name would be included.

"Would you be interested in taking part in our fund-raising?" Christine asked, though her tone was more polite than sincere. She sounded as though she hoped Caprice would decline.

"I'd love it! When do we start?"

"See?" Luke said proudly. "Didn't I tell you Caprice is full of enthusiasm?"

Christine gave her sister-in-law a reserved smile. "Yes, you did say that."

Caprice could hardly believe her good fortune. This could solve the entire problem!

"We'll meet next week and go over the list of names and how much money we're talking about. Judging by the Pin Oak show, we should have some idea how much we can expect since this will appeal to the same group of benefactors. Can you come to my house at, say, three o'clock on Tuesday of next week?"

"I certainly can! I can't tell you how strongly I'm behind this idea."

Christine studied her for a moment before she said, "Perhaps I've misjudged you. I had no idea you'd be interested in a project like this."

"Why would you assume that?"

"You haven't joined any clubs or backed any other charities that I know of."

Caprice smiled, "You can count on me to be squarely behind this one."

"Excellent." Christine stood up and said, "I have to be running now. Winston is expecting me home. We're going to the ballet tonight. Are you two going?"

Luke looked over at Caprice and grinned. "One thing Caprice and I have in common is a dislike of ballet. We won't be going."

Christine shook her head. "I don't know where we got you, Luke. You aren't like any of the Bannings."

Caprice put her arm around him and said, "He's exactly the way I want him."

Again Christine looked at Caprice as if she were reappraising her sister-in-law. "You know, it's hardly a secret that the family objected to your marriage, but I think we may have been wrong. You two do seem to be right for each other." She held out her hand to Caprice. "I love Luke, too. I want him to be happy." With a smile, she headed for the door. "Don't get up. I'll see myself out."

With a look of amazement on her face, Caprice watched Christine leave. Luke whispered, "See? I told you they would come around."

She put her arms around him. "Do you have any idea how much I love you?"

"How much?" he teased.

"More than anything."

"Show me."

With a smile she guided him down the hall toward their bedroom. "Luke, if you ever found out something, well, upsetting about me—would you still love me?"

Thoughts of the man named Jed Farnell that Luke had been trying to close out of his mind were instantly resurrected. He carefully examined his feelings before answering her. "I will always love you. How could I help it? But trust is very important to me.

There are some things I don't know if I could stand."
He knew she had been out, but he wouldn't let himself believe that it was to see Farnell. However, his
conscious mind was at odds with the jealousy that tore
at him.

"There is something I want to tell you. Something
you need to know," she said as they reached the bedroom.

A cold dread poured over him. Paulette had used
almost the same words when she told him about one
of her lovers. "No!" he said harshly. Caprice looked
up at him in surprise.

He took her face between his hands and gazed deep
into her eyes. "Don't hurt me, Caprice. Let there be
secrets between us if that will preserve our happiness.
Confessions aren't necessarily good for a marriage."

She was confused, but she nodded. He must suspect she wasn't the person she pretended to be and
didn't want his suspicions confirmed. She wondered
what slip had given her away, but she knew she must
make dozens of tiny mistakes every day.

He bent and kissed her hungrily, as if he were afraid
their love might not last. A bittersweet longing
touched her. After only this short a time as his wife
and lover, she couldn't bear the idea that it all might
end. "Luke," she whispered, "don't ever make me go
away."

Again he kissed her, his mouth silencing anything
else she might say. Caprice leaned into his embrace
and enjoyed the feel of his hard length against her.
When their lips parted, she said, "Make love with me.
Now."

He scooped her up and carried her to the bed. For a minute their gazes met and she saw an emotion she couldn't name in the smoky depths of his eyes.

"I'll never agree to share you," he said huskily. "I don't want anything to take you away from me."

Thinking he meant the time she would be spending with Christine's charity project, Caprice smiled. "I understand, Luke."

He laid her on the bed and removed her clothes before taking off his own, his hot eyes devouring her sensuous body. "You're like a dream," he said as he stretched out beside her. "Your skin seems to glow like marble and your hair is like pale fire." He ran his fingers through it wonderingly. "If it didn't have a touch of red, it would be almost platinum. I've never seen hair this color."

She breathed happily at the love she saw on his face. "No matter what else I do, I'll always have time for us to do this."

He looked at her strangely, but she lifted her head and ran the tip of her tongue over his shoulder. Her hands stroked the firm muscles of his back and arms. "Every time I touch you, I want you more. I love your taste and your smell and your texture." She licked the skin across his chest and sighed with pleasure.

"Caprice," he murmured, "never leave me."

"Never," she echoed softly as their lips met again.

Luke's hand stroked her breast, and Caprice felt the familiar, yet ever new, excitement within her. As his fingers toyed with her nipple the pleasurable sensation went straight to the center of her being.

She moved against him and felt the hardness that meant he was as excited as she was. Her own desire raged, and she parted her legs to draw him closer.

Although she urged him on with murmured words and caresses, he held back until she trembled beneath him. His hand moved lower and Caprice sighed his name as he touched the wellspring of her desire.

With a knowing smile he stroked her, bringing her ever higher in her need for him. Caprice felt as fragile as a bubble as he played on her senses and strummed her to an ecstasy that she couldn't control.

As her desire rushed to its summit, he entered her and she cried out as the hot waves washed through her.

The pulsing of her body gradually subsided and she opened her eyes to meet his intense gaze. "I love you," he said as he continued moving deep within her.

She matched his long, sure strokes and felt a sheen of sweat slick their skin as excitement again built between them. His stormy eyes darkened as he neared his climax, and Caprice felt a surge of love for him that was so intense it was almost painful. "I love you, Luke," she said as she again reached her completion. A second later he gripped her tightly as he, too, found fulfillment.

Caprice was cradled in the mellow glow of afterlove and enjoyed the security of his arms about her. Surely nothing could destroy her world when they had so much love between them.

Caprice arrived promptly at Christine's house on the day of the charity meeting. She rang the bell, and as she waited for someone to open the door, she smoothed her skirt and checked to be sure her blouse was neatly tucked into the waistband. Making a good first impression on these ladies was important, especially since this probably was not the first time some of them had seen her.

She self-consciously touched her hair. Since these were Christine's friends, it was likely that some of them had been to Christine's wedding reception and would have seen Caprice in her Sunny Day caterer's uniform before she dyed her hair brown. Her natural hair color was so distinctive, she was concerned that one of them might remember it and her face as well. But she hoped the drastic difference between seeing her as a waitress and as a wealthy socialite would confuse them sufficiently that they would not be sure the two were the same person.

The door opened, and Christine's butler escorted her to the living room, where Christine introduced her to the others. A gaunt woman with her hair done up in a sleek black bun greeted her with icy politeness, and a peculiar expression, and Caprice wondered if the woman, Philippa Hadley, recognized her. She was relieved when the woman said, rather acidly, "I know Luke *quite* well. It's so... nice to meet his wife." The woman's aloofness was apparently only due to jealousy.

"Ladies," Christine said, "let's get down to business."

Caprice sat on a rose sofa beside a woman who was balancing a small saucer of finger sandwiches and fish-shaped crackers on her knee. As she looked at the others, she noticed that several of them seemed to have been staring at her. But none showed any sign of recognition, and Caprice drew a deep, calming breath.

"As you know," Christine said, "we have a lot to do today. Philippa is in charge of setting up the polo match." Everyone glanced at the dark-haired woman and smiled their appreciation.

Philippa gave a brief run-down of her activities thus far, and Caprice was genuinely impressed. Where, she wondered, did one go to learn how to arrange a polo match? Evidently Philippa knew how to rise to the challenge, because she had already located two teams willing to put on an exhibition match and was hot on the trail of a suitable field.

"That's marvelous," Christine said, as if she had expected no less. "We have here the names referred to us by the doctors we contacted. I have arranged them alphabetically, and I suggest we go over them one by one." She put on pale pink reading glasses and added, "I am assuming we will raise something in the neighborhood of a million dollars from the polo match. Considering the high cost of medical care, my guess is we'll be able to pick five or six from the list."

Caprice felt her mouth go dry as Christine read out the first name and the child's medical problem. The list was long, and after each name there was a discussion as to whether or not that child's need was greater than the others.

She looked about the room at the elegantly attired ladies who were gathered there to play God. How could they decide which child to support and which to refuse? For a minute her old feelings of hostility returned, but as she considered something Luke had told her soon after they met, her emotions evened out. He had said that the poor were always there. For every child on the list, there were hundreds of others, thousands even, with needs just as dire. As rich as these people were, they couldn't hope to help them all.

When she heard Christine reading Heather's name, her attention was jerked back to the room. She was on the list!

As she had with the others, Christine read Heather's diagnosis and Dr. Granger's prognosis.

"She has two parents," an elderly woman commented. "Are they employed?"

Christine consulted her notes. "The mother is; apparently the father is not. Thus far the doctor has been paid for only the first two visits."

Caprice frowned. What had Katie done with the rest of the money she had given her? Paying a phone bill and buying a refrigerator wouldn't take four thousand dollars!

"It seems to me the father could go to work and the family not be in a financial bind."

"The doctor requires half the money up front," Caprice said. "A hundred thousand is a lot of money, especially in a lump sum."

All the eyes in the room swiveled toward her.

"I read that somewhere," Caprice added lamely.

"She's correct about that," Christine said. "The transplant she needs will cost two hundred thousand and the administrative staffs of all the hospitals who provide these kinds of operations insist that half be paid in advance."

"How long does the doctor give this child?" Philippa asked.

"It says here she may need the operation within the year. That's not as urgent as some."

"But it may be sooner," said Caprice, who knew Dr. Granger had recently reevaluated Heather's case and was now saying that she had six months at the outside. "Sometimes the children don't respond to the medication and the operation is required sooner than expected."

"Yes, I'm sure that's true in all these cases," Christine said. "The next name is . . ."

Caprice didn't listen. From the way Dr. Granger had presented Heather's case, she didn't seem to be in as desperate a situation as Caprice knew she was. Nervously she waited until Christine had gone through the entire list.

"Some of these we can eliminate right away," Christine said. She drew lines through the names of those who were either in the higher income brackets or whose disease was developing slowly.

A discussion followed as the women tried to determine which names to discard and which to keep. Each case was evaluated as to the urgency of the need and the estimated cost. At last the list was narrowed down to six, and Heather was one of them.

"I think we should strike the Farnell girl in favor of the little boy with kidney problems," the elderly woman said.

"I don't," Caprice spoke up. "The boy with the bad kidneys can be treated with dialysis, but there isn't a machine to do what the liver does." She hated hear-

ing the words come out of her mouth. Who was she to
say that boy shouldn't have new kidneys?

"I think we should bump them both and put on the
three-year-old that needs a heart transplant," a blond
woman said. "Even though her parents make more
money than these others, the operation is also more
expensive." Looking at Caprice, she added, "There's
no dialysis for the heart, either."

"Please reconsider Heather Farnell," Caprice said.
"I think her case is more serious than you realize."

"Why on earth would you assume that?" Philippa
said with thinly veiled animosity.

"Call it intuition," Caprice said.

Several of the ladies smiled at the newcomer's ec-
centricity.

Christine said, "It's getting late, ladies. Let's bring
it to a vote."

Five minutes later Caprice was on her way home.
The boy named Todd Brown was going to get new
kidneys, and the girl named Heather Farnell was going
to have to make do with her own liver.

"How did it go?" Luke asked when she came in the
door.

"Christine and the others were pleased."

"You weren't?"

"I feel sick when I think of it. We sat around like
the Fates and decided who would be helped and who
wouldn't. Luke, I feel dirty. I actually suggested a little boy with failing kidneys could wait for an operation! I had no right to do that!"

He pulled her down beside him on the couch and
put his arms around her. "You can't save them all,

honey. At least there are a few that have a chance now that wouldn't have had one before.''

She nodded as her eyes filled with tears. That was true, but one of them wasn't named Heather Farnell, and Heather's time was running out.

Chapter Fourteen

Luke, I have to talk to you," Ralph said. "In private."

Caprice looked up from her sketches as Luke left the room. "What do you have to say to me that you couldn't say in front of Caprice?" he asked testily.

"Come to the office with me, please."

Luke followed the man down the corridor and closed them into the privacy of his office. "This had better be good, Ralph. I don't like the obvious rudeness with which you excluded Caprice just then. She's my wife, damn it, and you'd better start accepting it."

"I just talked to Morris Ainsley."

"The investigator? I told you to call him off!"

"I did, but he had already sent out a trace on Jed Farnell. It came in today, and he called to tell me about it.

"Oh?" Luke's eyes narrowed dangerously.

"Farnell has been in prison in Louisiana. It seems he was conning some elderly couple and was convicted for it. He got out last June on good behavior."

"Are you sure?"

"Ainsley said he would send over the information if we request it, including the name of the couple and the exact details of the scam."

"Yes. Do that."

Ralph moved uneasily. "I hate to say it, but there's something else."

Luke glared at him.

"Last month when Pablo was setting out those new shrubs, he saw a man that fits Farnell's description pull up out front and park. He was driving an old Ford. He said your wife stepped out to meet him before the man rang the bell and that before he left she gave him money."

A pounding anger started in Luke's temples. He recalled the day quite well—he had almost collided with Farnell as he turned in the drive. Caprice had said the man had been there to apply for the position of gardener. She had lied.

Back in the sunroom, Caprice was distinctly uneasy over the way Ralph had called Luke out of the room. She considered going to Ralph's office and demanding that she be included in whatever he had to say since it evidently was about her. Before she could leave the room, she heard the phone ring. Without waiting for Lawford to get it, she picked it up, and when she recognized Katie's voice, she sat bolt upright. Something must be terribly wrong for her to call.

"Cappy, Heather has taken a turn for the worse. She's really bad sick. The doctor has found a liver donor, but we have to do something immediately. If not . . . what should I do?"

Caprice pressed her fingertips to her forehead. "This is so sudden! What happened?"

"I don't know. She wasn't feeling well yesterday morning so I kept her in bed, but by suppertime her fever went so high I took her to the hospital. I've never seen her so sick! Dr. Granger thinks we may . . . lose her." Katie's voice broke into sobbing tears. "Cappy, I'm so scared! You've got to come down and bring the money."

"But I don't have . . ." Caprice's voice trailed off as her eyes locked onto the books that hid the wall safe.

"You have to! You can't let us down now! God, Caprice, what kind of a person are you?"

She heard hysteria rising in Katie's voice so she said, "Calm down. Does Dr. Granger still insist on having half the money up front?"

"Of course he does!"

Caprice made a decision. "All right. Tell him I'm on my way with the money."

She hung up and resolutely went to the safe. She had no idea how much money was in it, but she knew it was a great deal. She hoped it was still there. Not letting herself think about whether this was stealing or not, Caprice deactivated the alarm and dialed the combination.

When she saw the stacks of one-hundred-dollar bills on the cold metal shelf where they had been before, her heart began to pound. Caprice took out one of the bundles marked with a band that indicated it was worth ten-thousand dollars and eyed it nervously before setting it aside. Five of these bundles, along with the money in the joint account, would cover the down payment for the operation. But what about the balance? When she forced her mind to slow down enough to think more rationally, she decided that since there was so much money in the safe, she had better get the other hundred thousand now. Luke was going to explode anyway. Quickly she grabbed ten more bundles, relocked the safe, and put the books back in place. As she was stuffing the last of the money bundles into her large over-the-shoulder bag, Luke came in.

She could see at a glance that he was furious, but she was sure he hadn't seen her take the money. Whatever Ralph had told him had clearly enraged him.

"Where are you going?" he demanded.

Thinking quickly, she held out her purse and gestured toward their bedroom. "I was about to put my purse away."

"I have some questions I want you to answer first." He stalked toward her, and she unconsciously took a step back. "Who is Jed Farnell?"

Cotton filled her mouth as she tried to smile. "Who?"

"Don't play games with me, Caprice! Who is he? Is he your lover?"

"What?" She was more astounded than afraid. "Of course not!"

"Then who is he to you? And don't bother to lie. I know you go to his house on Bixby Street."

Her eyes widened in amazement. "How do you know that?"

"So you don't even try to deny it! You amaze me, Caprice. You really do. I could have sworn you loved me. I swallowed all your lies as fast as you could tell them to me. You and Farnell must have really enjoyed that."

"No, Luke, you're wrong. I do love you. I'm not having an affair with anyone—and certainly not with Jed."

"I'm not so sure I believe you, but if it's not an affair—God! How civilized that word sounds for a creep like that!"

"You've seen him?" she asked in confusion.

"Oh, yes. I saw him leaving here the day he 'applied for a gardener's job.' Remember? You weren't very convincing, but I believed the whole thing."

"I'm telling you there is nothing like that between us. Nothing at all!"

"No? Then it must be something a bit more lucrative. Like fleecing me of my money, perhaps. I called Wellesley College, and no Caprice Dolan was ever registered there. I also checked about a fire in The

Woodlands, and none was reported within the year. Not even the one that burned your sister's clothes and required that you give her yours. You have a lot of explaining to do, and you're staying right here until you do it!''

Caprice opened her mouth, but she couldn't find the words. She had never seen Luke so angry. Fury seemed to snap and crackle all around him. In his present mood she doubted she could make him understand. Suddenly she felt the bulk of the money in her purse and realized at the very least he would prevent her from getting it to Heather.

Taking a steadying breath, she said, "I can explain everything, Luke."

"I hope so for your sake. I also found out your fine friend has been serving time in Louisiana so don't try to whitewash him."

A flicker of surprise lit Caprice's eyes.

"Didn't he tell you? Maybe he's switched his game from con artist to embezzler. Sit down and start talking."

"I'll explain everything, but first I have to get something out of our room."

"What?" he demanded.

"Please, Luke, let me do this my own way. I'll only be a minute."

She hurried down the hall to the bedroom and closed the door. Panic assailed her, but she had no choice. Whatever happened to her, she had to save Heather. She opened the patio door that led to the pool and sneaked through Pablo's carefully tended flower beds so Luke wouldn't see her from the sunroom, then she broke into a run for her car. The engine roared to life, and she drove away.

Luke paced furiously. He couldn't think of anything but Caprice and Jed Farnell. After a while his mind cleared enough for him to notice the books that hid the wall safe. He always lined up the spines with the front edge of the shelf, but now the books were pushed all the way in.

"Caprice!" he called out as he went to the books. "Caprice, come in here!" He checked the alarm system and found it was turned off. For a painful moment he paused. Had he caught her taking money from the safe? Was that why she had looked so startled?

He opened the safe and was relieved to see there was still money there. Quickly he counted it, then counted it again. One hundred and fifty thousand dollars was missing! Why would she take that much and leave the rest? Unless she thought he would be less likely to miss it that way.

Again anger wrenched at him. He had been made a fool of again! "Caprice!" he yelled as he strode down the hall.

The bedroom was empty, and through the patio door he saw her footprints clearly embedded in the flower garden. Luke ran outside, but her car was gone as well. Deep pain tore at him, and he felt almost nauseated. Caprice had proved to be even worse than Paulette.

On leaden feet, Luke went back into the bedroom they had shared, and sat on the bed where they had loved. He could still picture her in the room, her bright hair flowing in waves over his pillow, her bubbling laughter making his life a paradise. And all the while she was playing him for a fool.

Luke buried his face in his trembling hands and tried not to love her.

All that night Caprice sat in the hospital waiting room with Katie and occasionally with Jed. Because of the urgency, Dr. Granger had started the operation as soon as possible. Caprice paid the hospital the one hundred and fifty thousand she had taken from the wall safe, and then wrote out a check for the other fifty thousand from the joint account checkbook.

As Katie watched, she noticed that her name was also on the imprinted check. "Caprice, why didn't you tell me about this account?"

Caprice debated her answer for a moment. Should she tell Katie she had decided she couldn't trust her with the money for Heather's care? What was the point? Katie wouldn't change, and besides, now that Heather's care was assured, there would be no more reason for her to deal with such large sums of money. Looking her sister squarely in the eye, Caprice said, "I thought I already had. I guess it slipped my mind. The important thing is that Heather is getting her transplant." To the clerk in the admissions office, Caprice said, "Please give the receipt to Mrs. Farnell."

While the receipt was being made out, Caprice returned to the waiting room. Jed was slouched in a chair across the smoke-filled room. He scowled at her, then looked away.

Caprice watched Katie come in, waver, then join Jed. She closed her eyes. This was going to be a long night.

Before dawn Jed stood abruptly. "I can't handle this," he said to Katie.

"I know," she said in a pitying voice. "It's hard on us all. Surely the doctor will come out soon and tell us how she is."

Jed paced to the hallway and back again. "You should have told me how bad off she was."

"We tried," Caprice said in a tired voice.

Jed ran a shaking hand through his hair. "I need a drink."

"Now?" Caprice asked, looking at him for the first time in hours.

"Yes, now! Maybe you can sit there all prim and proper, but this is tearing me up inside. That's my baby girl in there! What if she don't make it?"

"She'll be all right, Jed," his wife soothed. "Dr. Granger said he has plenty of confidence in her being able to pull through."

"What if it don't take? You hear about things like that." Neither woman had an answer, so he said, "Give me some money, Katie. Come on, give it to me!"

Reluctantly Katie fished several folded bills out of her purse and handed them to Jed. "Where are you going?"

"To get a drink, I said! Don't grill me!" He strode out and was gone.

"Do you think he's coming back?" Katie asked in a small voice.

"How much money did you give him?"

"About a hundred dollars."

Caprice sighed and shook her head in resignation. That plus the money he'd blackmailed out of her would take him a long way. "I imagine he will, eventually."

Katie sat opposite her sister and said, "I know you hate him, but you don't know him like I do. He means to do right. He just can't take pressure. This with Heather, well, it's been too much for him."

Caprice studied her sister as if Katie were a stranger. "I'll never understand what you see in him."

"He's like a little boy in some ways. I guess part of him never grew up. But I love him."

Caprice nodded. The description also fit Katie. "You deserve better than Jed has to give."

"Well, we can't all marry Luke Bannings," Katie said defensively.

"And we can't all stay married to them, either."

"What's that supposed to mean?"

"It means I can't go back home. Are my old clothes still at your house?"

"Yes. Heather has been using that room since you left, but she just pushed your clothes to the back. Are you moving back in with us?"

"No. I don't know what I'm going to do yet, but we can't go back to the way we were."

"I know. But at least the plan worked. Heather got her operation."

"Yes. The plan worked." Caprice wondered if that was all Katie really could see, or if she didn't care that her sister's marriage was over. Perhaps Katie's jealousy had been even greater than Caprice had thought.

She waited until the exhausted doctor came out to tell them Heather was alive and in the recovery room, then she went home with Katie for a much needed rest.

Luke knocked, then banged on the front door of the house on Bixby Street. Three children too young to go to school—and also too young to play unattended so near the street—watched him in wide-eyed silence. Luke frowned at the door and banged on it again. There was no sound from within, and he wasn't surprised. This was his third visit and the result had always been the same.

"Do you kids know the man who lives here?" he demanded.

The children turned and ran away with staccato shrieks. Luke scowled. He hadn't meant to frighten them. He tried knocking at the house next door since the children had fled into that yard, but either no one was home or no one was willing to open the door.

Luke went back to his car and sat for a moment gazing at the house. He couldn't imagine Caprice in this setting.

He was tired to the bone, and it took a conscious effort to start the car and drive home. In the three days since Caprice had been gone, he had hardly slept at all. Ralph had encouraged him to call the police to report the missing money, and Luke had been hard pressed not to knock him down on the spot. As it was, he was looking for a replacement for his longtime financial manager.

Where could she be? The question haunted him day and night. After twenty-four hours had passed, he had reported her as missing, but so far no word of her whereabouts had been called in. Was she with Jed Farnell? The idea made Luke sick.

He dragged himself into his house and dropped onto the couch. Without Caprice there, it seemed so damned empty. He wondered if he could find her and convince her to come home. Despite his hurt and anger, he wanted her back again. His love for Caprice was stronger than his pride. He knew she had a good reason for all this. She had to.

When the phone rang, he was tempted to ignore it. Lawford would answer the extension and Luke could say he wouldn't talk to anyone. On the other hand, it might be the police with news of Caprice.

"Hello?"

"I was beginning to think you weren't home," Christine said. "What's going on with you these days?"

Luke gritted his teeth. He didn't want his family to know anything about his problems until he knew for certain that Caprice wouldn't be coming back. "Not much," he said gruffly.

"Is Caprice there?"

"Why?"

"There's no need to snap at me, Luke. I just wanted to give her the good news. Another club has volunteered to pay for a kidney operation for the little boy on our list, so we can include the little girl she wanted."

"What?" This was so far from his mind he couldn't figure out what Christine was talking about.

"The charity list. You know, for the polo match?"

"Oh, that."

"Anyway, Caprice was very strong on including a little girl named Heather Farnell, who has a bad liver, and—"

"What did you say?" Luke leaned forward excitedly.

"She has a bad liver."

"No, no. What was her name?"

"Heather Farnell."

"Farnell!" The coincidence was great, but still...

"She was recommended by Dr. Eugene Granger. The case didn't sound very immediate to me, but it seemed to touch Caprice. Is she there?"

"No, not now." He was busy writing the doctor's name on a notepad.

"You will tell her, won't you? I think she'll be pleased."

"Yes, yes. I'll tell her. Goodbye." He hung up and grabbed the phone book. Soon he was dialing Granger's office.

Caprice shifted in the uncomfortable chair in the intensive care waiting room. There was really no need for her to be at the hospital continuously, but she was as satisfied to be here as anywhere. She couldn't force herself to stay in Katie's house with the new and unpleasant memories it now held. Also she was afraid Jed would return, and she didn't want to be found there alone.

Each day after seeing Heather during the short morning visiting hours, Katie went to work, then returned that evening for another visit. Caprice stayed available for the five minutes she could see Heather after midday. That afternoon Heather had been alert enough to complain about the network of tubes and wires that connected her to glucose and various monitors. The nurse had privately admitted that this was a good sign.

Caprice looked down at her faded jeans and T-shirt. They were in great contrast to the emerald and diamond wedding ring she still wore on her left hand, but she couldn't force herself to take it off. After three nights of sleeping in her cramped and faintly musty room at Katie's, Caprice had begun to think of her brief marriage as a poignantly sweet dream. Cinderella had come home from the ball.

She slid lower on the plastic seat and wondered what she was going to do with her life. Katie had offered to let her live at the house, but Caprice couldn't do it. There were feelings between her sister and herself that Caprice couldn't even try to resolve at the present time. Bringing them out into the open would lead to words that might never be forgiven or forgotten. Until Caprice could become less emotional about the issues, it was better to let Katie bury their differences along with Jed's transgressions. Caprice would never be able to forget.

She missed Luke more than she had thought possible. Her ache for him went beyond mere longing—she *needed* him. She wanted to see his smile and hear the soft drawl of his voice. Caprice didn't dare allow herself to recall their lovemaking. The absence of just the small things were almost unbearable.

Glancing at the large clock on the wall, she sighed. Katie would be here soon. They would talk about Heather's improvement or the weather or world events but would carefully avoid any reference to the Sunny Day Caterers's bookings in River Oaks. Katie would go in to see her daughter. Then they would go home. Caprice would again feign exhaustion to avoid having to talk, and Katie would again try not to look relieved. Caprice wondered how many more days and nights like this she could live through.

Footsteps sounded on the tile floor of the corridor, but Caprice didn't turn her head. For the last three days she had imagined Luke's tread in every footfall. She was tired of looking up in anticipation only to meet disappointment.

The footsteps came into the waiting room and stopped beside her chair. Caprice found herself looking down at a pair of immaculately polished men's dress shoes. Her eyes traveled up the sharp crease in the chino trousers and over the red knit shirt to meet Luke's steady eyes.

He looked tired. There were lines near his eyes and at the corners of his mouth. She had seen the same creases of exhaustion in her own mirror.

"Well?" he said in a tight voice.

Caprice stood and clasped her hands in front of her to keep from throwing her arms around him. "Well what?" she asked inanely. There was so much to say that she didn't know where to start.

"When you left the room—three days ago—you said you could explain. Let's hear it."

"Jed Farnell is my brother-in-law. He and my sister, Katie, have a daughter named Heather."

"Christine called me today and mentioned a Heather Farnell who needed a liver transplant."

"That's my niece. I tried to get her name on the list of charity beneficiaries, but she wasn't included. As it turned out, she couldn't wait that long anyway. I had to steal the money from you to pay the hospital, but I'll pay it back. It's going to take me a while, but I'll do it."

"Caprice—"

"No, let me finish. I have to say it all. This is who I really am," she said as she gestured at her faded jeans. "I'm not the Walters' niece, and I've never even been near Wellesley College. I wangled my way onto your yacht, and I did all I could to make you want to marry me because I saw no other way to pay for Heather's operation."

"You could have simply asked me."

"Sure, you always give two hundred thousand dollars to every stranger that asks nicely. Who wouldn't?" She motioned for him to let her continue. "As soon as Heather was well, I was going to tell you everything and let you divorce me. I wasn't going to ask for any settlement at all—I really wasn't, but I guess you won't believe that now. Only—" she paused and drew a deep breath "—only something happened that I didn't expect. I fell in love with you."

She walked across the room as she tried to control herself. She couldn't break down and cry now, even though the tears were so close. There would be plenty of time for that later, when she was alone in her room at Katie's. Luke's eyes followed her intently.

"I fell in love with you," she repeated as she returned to him. "I love you more than life itself. All at once what I was doing seemed so wrong, yet I was in too deep to stop."

She knotted her fingers together to stop their trembling. "Then Jed came home. He had deserted Katie and Heather over a year ago, and that wasn't the first time. As a matter of fact, he's gone again. He found out I had married you under false pretenses, and he began blackmailing me. I *was* going to tell you the truth, but I couldn't do it until Heather was safe."

"Couldn't you have trusted me that much?"

"Her life was at stake. If I was wrong about you, she would die. I couldn't risk it."

"Go on."

"That's about it. Katie and I had words over Jed because she won't ever believe anything bad about him. I returned the furs and jewels you bought me, and I took the rest of the money from the wall safe."

"Yes, I know." He took her left hand and looked down at the sparkling wedding ring. "Why didn't you sell this? It's worth quite a bit."

"I couldn't," she said softly. "Not my wedding ring." She started to pull it off to return it to him.

Luke closed his hand over hers. "Leave it there." He looked at her for a minute without speaking, as if he were carefully choosing his words. "At first I thought you and Farnell were having an affair. That's why I was so upset. After I talked to Christine, I had the crazy thought that Heather might even be your child by him."

"That would be a neat trick, since I was a virgin when you married me."

"I said it was a crazy thought. Then I figured out where you must be after I traced Heather here." He hesitated. "Now what do we do about all this?"

"I don't know. I guess Ralph will be more than happy to arrange our divorce." Her voice wavered on the last word. "I won't contest it or ask for anything."

"Do you want a divorce?"

"No." She stared up at him. "I really think we should have one though."

"Why?"

"I married you under false pretenses!"

"When did you start to love me?"

"I think it started on your yacht the night of the party. That's why I left so quickly. I was afraid if I stayed, there would be no need for you to marry me."

"Then you loved me before we were married? That doesn't sound very false to me. Do you still love me?"

"Yes. Luke, why torment me like this? I've said you can have a divorce. Isn't that enough?"

"No, it isn't. It's not nearly enough."

"Why not?"

"Because I love you."

"But I stole—"

"A wife can't steal from her own husband. This is a community-property state."

"Well, I *lied*."

"That's not grounds for divorce."

Caprice stared up at him. Incredulously she asked, "Are you saying you want me back?"

"Yes, and I won't take no for an answer. If I have to court you all over again, I will. I don't want to lose you. We love each other. We can't just throw away something that precious."

She was so surprised that she couldn't think of what to say.

"Well?" he asked impatiently. "Are you coming home or not?"

"Yes!" Caprice threw her arms around him, and didn't care who saw them.

"Would you just look at that?" one nurse said to another. "Those rich people think they own the world. Carrying on like that in public."

"I'll say. I bet neither one of them ever did a lick of real work or had a worry in their lives!" the other nurse snorted.

Caprice laughed softly as Luke's lips closed over hers.

*   *   *   *   *